THE MAN WITH THE HOLE IN HIS HEAD

KEVIN WOOLRIDGE

THE MAN WITH THE HOLE IN HIS HEAD

KEVIN WOOLRIDGE

ENGEN BOOKS

Published in Canada by Engen Books, St. John's, NL.

Library and Archives Canada Cataloguing in Publication

Woolridge, Kevin, 1977-
The man with the hole in his head / Kevin Woolridge.

Also issued in electronic format.

ISBN 978-1-926903-08-8

I. Title.
PS8645.O6583M36 2012 C813'.6 C2012-904194-7

Distributed by:
Engen Books
38 Pearson Street, Suite 149
St. John's NL A1A 3R1
www.engenbooks.com
info@engenbooks.com

First mass market paperback printing: August 2012
First mass market digital publication: August 2012

Cover Photo: Joey Woolridge

For my Aunt Shirley,
who gave me my first typewriter
and for my parents,
who encouraged me to use it.

The city didn't have a name. Not officially anyway. In 1893 when the city was incorporated, it wasn't allowed to keep its name. It wasn't even allowed to choose a new one. An odd law and odder still that none of its residents questioned it. The City Hall was called simply *City Hall*; same with the *City Library*, *City Bank* and *City Hospital*. The old town name was forgotten; erased from the memories of its citizens. Times were booming and they had no reason to complain; gold one decade and oil the next. Money rolling in faster than it could be spent. Industry and all the conveniences of the modern age just around the corner.

Up until the nineteen sixties the city was just a dot on the map, fifty miles northwest of Chicago. It was an enigma; a curiosity; a fun fact to read about at the bottom of the weekend paper; something to tell the tourists. *Did you know there is a city without a name? Go ahead. Look on the map. See that dot. Nothing next to it. No it's not a printing error.* People in the Big Onion called it North City and in 1963 some brilliant cartographer decided to put that name on a map. It was the same year the big tornado hit, taking with it thirteen houses, four buses and ten cows. Not to mention dogs, cats, post office boxes, fences, abandoned shopping carts and one sports mascot, furry costume and all. Most of it landed in Chi-town. The mascot was never found. Though some said that if you rolled your window down late at night on the Kennedy Expressway you could hear the faint chanting of *de-fence! de-fence*! in the distance. The new map was recalled and changed, strictly to preserve the historical oddity. Certainly not because of a fear of supernatural repercussions. Cartographers are many things, superstitious is not one of them. Nobody called it North City anymore, not even when asking for directions on the interstate. It was The Dot. As in *dot on a map*. And since it was a nickname the old law wasn't being broken. You see, in 1893, a town about to become a city, a town about to get everything it ever needed or wanted, signed its charter in blood.

1

The little electronics store clock started beeping, its red letters flashing twelve zero zero PM. It was about time to get up out of bed. About time to put on some pants, throw down some cereal and forget absolutely everything that happened the night before. Camper King rolled over, slapped his hand down on the clock and sat up on the edge of his bed. He lifted his shirt, a grey tee with a worn logo that may have once been a cow and checked for new wounds; nothing visible. Just the regular half healed scars and faded bruises. He checked his hands next. No blood or hair under the fingernails and every finger and adjacent knuckle still in place. He took a deep breath. Well, either things had gone perfectly last night or else horribly wrong. He put his money on perfectly, since *horribly wrong* would have had him waking up in a ditch; a ditch on the road to hell. Luckily he didn't remember a thing about it. The only good side effect of the whole business. And if memory loss was a good side effect you could only imagine the bad ones.

He stood up slowly and a beam of light from the window caught him in the face. He wasn't a particularly handsome man, but he had all the features that should have made him handsome; a strong jaw, chiseled chin, deep eyes and hair that hinted at a boyish, innocent quality, but everything about him seemed worn down like a rusty statue or a hotel suite that had seen one too many parties. Camper winced, pulled the curtain tight and tried to find his sunglasses.

Not on the table and not on the floor. Not under any clothes and definitely not in his coat pocket. He must have left them at the job. Well, it wouldn't have been the first time that's for sure and probably wouldn't be the last time. The glasses were cheap and available pretty much anywhere. He threw some jeans on and headed to the kitchen, closing curtains along the way.

"...in another serial killing last night. Religious objects located at the scene have-"

Camper switched the channel. He hated the news. Wile E. Coyote suited his tastes much better. Even in black and white on his little twelve inch kitchen TV. He often woke up feeling like someone had dropped an anvil on his head from the top of a cliff and secretly he wished some day that the coyote would catch the road runner. Catch him and barbeque him. He munched his Capt'n Crunch getting milk on his chin. He actually preferred it warm and soggy, but he was too tired to boil the kettle.

"...police officials warn that the killer or killers is still at large. Margaret French reporting."

Wait a second. What happened to Wile E Coyote? He didn't remember changing the channel. Everything was the same. He was still eating his cereal. The milk dripping from his spoon.

"Margaret, are there any indications that this is a change in behavior for the killer."

Camper perked up. This was getting serious.

"No. Not necessarily, Bob. Although this is the first time that a child has been killed."

He dropped his spoon. It fell almost in slow motion, drowning an eyelash that had fallen into the bowl.

"Our prayers are with the family tonight. Thank you Margaret. And now on to the weather. Looks like we're in for some rough-"

Someone wanted him to see that. Someone wanted him to know. But that wasn't the way the whole thing worked. He did a job and then he forgot it. That's how it was supposed to happen. There was no going back. But someone or something had changed the channel. And changed the channel for a reason. Some supernatural force had wanted him to know that a child was dead. A child was dead and he probably did it. A child was dead and that shouldn't have happened. Camper King was gonna find out why. Come hell or high water. Or both.

The newspapers said pretty much the same thing.

PENTAGRAM KILLER STILL AT LARGE.

YOUNG GIRL KILLED IN RITUAL MURDER.

Camper hated the moniker but there was nothing he could do about it. He'd been playing the game for a while now, but only recently was it making it into the papers. Maybe he was slipping. He had every paper he could find spread out on the table and the news channel on all day. He had to remember what happened. If he was losing he had to know. He had to know that he was still in control. If he had lost himself then the war was already over.

Last night, according to investigators, somewhere between the hours of twelve and two, three men, a woman and a young girl were murdered in an industrial park warehouse. Lead Investigator Vanessa Gamby has said it was likely the five were bound and taken from their homes to the warehouse. She believes the Pentagram Killer is behind this incident. "We found traces of garlic, salt and what we believe to be holy water. A pentagram was painted on the floor where the victims were found." The five have yet to be identified.

Not much there. Garlic, salt and holy water. He got up and went to the cupboard. Sure enough he was running low. He hated the smell of garlic himself and didn't like having to buy it. Running from store to store, buying a bit here and there so as not to arouse suspicion. But who would be suspicious of a guy buying garlic in pounds? Well, everyone who read the paper now. Holy water wasn't so bad since he could do it himself. After ten years that still freaked him out. At least he didn't have to wear the collar. And the pentagram? God only knew. Either he drew it or they did. Could have been either.

His head hurt; a slow dull throb creeping over his skull and into the back of his eyes. Great. The headaches were starting. That was all he needed. He popped a few pills and looked out the window. The sun was finally going down. He grabbed his coat and headed out the door, not even bothering to lock it. It was just one of those days.

At the end of his road was an odd little store called *American Style Convenience*. He didn't really understand what that meant, but they had everything he needed and were dead cheap. He didn't exactly get paid very well for his services and didn't care much for brand names anyways. Except for one.

"Just a Cherry Coke, Phil."

Camper smiled at the owner. Nice enough fella. Worked almost all the store shifts himself. At least Camper had never been served by anyone but Phil. He looked nervous tonight. His eyes were shifty.

"Everything alright Phil?"

"Oh yeah. Yeah. Everything's great you know. Everything's great."

Something was definitely wrong. Everything was great? That didn't suit the owner of a convenience store. No matter *how* good business was Phil usually had something to say about late deliveries or city politics or at the very least a word of apology for the kids hanging outside. Come to think of it there weren't any kids hanging outside either. Damn odd for a store in the 'burbs. Even on a school night. Phil's hands were shaking as he took Camper's money. His smile was cracked. And he was sweating. Camper's instincts cut in.

"I've got to get one more thing."

"Sure sure."

He moved back down one of the aisles, deliberately keeping the corner of his eye on the counter. He moved slowly, pretending to look for something when he caught a glimpse of movement on the CCTV monitor that wasn't his. He had been sure the store was empty when he came in. He picked up a large can of peas and started back to the counter. There was someone else there. That was for certain. And Phil's *American Style Convenience* was being *American Style* robbed. No way was someone messing with his local corner store. Not after the day he had been having. That just wasn't right.

He approached the counter slowly, holding the can of peas up and smiling.

"I forgot the peas."

"Oh yeah. That happens. Sure sure."

He laid the can on the counter and handed Phil another dollar, knocking the canned peas to the floor with a deft flick of the wrist.

"Whoops."

With a smile he bent down to pick it up.

"That was lucky Phil. I didn't even notice that my shoelace was untied. I might have broken my neck on the way out. Let me just tie it up here. "

Camper King had a doctorate in stalling and a masters in misdirection. Both were important in his line of work. He made his way slowly around the counter, talking all the while, the tin can of peas raised in his hand.

"So what do you think about this Pentagram Killer business, Phil? Pretty nasty stuff hey. I wouldn't worry about it if I were you. You've got nothing to be worried about. Gotcha!"

A little punk with a knife about the size of a nail file was bent down behind the counter. When Camper came around the corner he looked about ready to shit himself. He raised the knife, as if to file his nails maybe, and Camper let the can of peas fly. It was all over in about ten seconds. A can of peas to the head will take out just about anybody.

Phil called the cops and Camper got free Cherry Cokes for life. The can of peas he left next to the register, with a dent in it. Better than a gun under the counter. It was a great start to the night. A good deed done and nothing supernatural about it. And it was a memory he would get to keep. No one was taking that one. He smiled to himself. A can of peas to the head. He'd have to use that one again some time. As he crossed the road he flicked open his can of Coke.

Unfortunately he didn't see the car coming.

2

Camper woke up in the back of an Emergency Van. Only the siren wasn't wailing. And his legs were bound. And the EMT was a tad too unshaven.

"King. King!"

"Huh?"

"King, this is a real problem."

"My legs?"

"No, no, you're legs are fine. Don't worry about your legs. No pain."

"Are we going to the hospital?" He was still feeling pretty shaken. Getting hit by a car and waking up bound by ropes can do that to a person. Camper had gone through some weird stuff, but that didn't mean he was used to it.

"No. No hospital. We're going to The Circle."

The EMT lifted his shirt and showed Camper the circular tattoo underneath. Great. Just when things were looking up. The van hit a few bumps and he realized they were driving on a dirt road. He had never been to the headquarters of The Circle, at least as far as he could remember, and it certainly wasn't something he had ever planned on doing. He felt a pinch on his arm and the fake

EMT sat up with a needle, smiling. His teeth were far too white. Everything went very bright and then very dark. And then he couldn't hear anything. And then the visions started.

He was standing on an empty road. There were no street lights. The moon was huge above him; a giant dinner plate in the sky. He tried walking, but he couldn't. His feet were stuck to the ground. The moon seemed to get bigger and loomed over him. And there were planets up there as well; Saturn and Jupiter and Mars, all huge and taking up the sky. Stars shot between them in showers and strange patterns appeared on their surfaces: spirals and lines and symbols he didn't recognize but that felt familiar. He was small; small and vulnerable. He felt suddenly that the world itself might tip like a boat and he'd just slide off the edge, eaten by the vastness below. It scared him. That he would just fall forever with nothing to latch onto, surrounded by darkness. Just as he thought it might actually happen, that the world itself was tipping, he felt a hand in his. A tiny hand. He looked down. It was a little girl. She held his hand tightly and looked up at him.

"Don't worry," she said. "You won't fall."

And then she died.

When Camper woke he was covered in sweat. The phony EMT was gone. He was sitting on a chair in an empty room and there was a circle drawn in chalk on the floor around him. His legs were free and so were his hands.

'Silly boys,' he thought, and got up, heading for the door. That's when the pain started, deep in his stomach.

Like someone had his intestines stuck in a meat grinder and were grinding slowly in preparation for sausage making. He sat back down and the pain subsided. Of course. The circle on the floor. Well, nothing to do but wait then. He wished he still had his Cherry Coke. He wished he had another can of peas. A big one. With a detonator.

Just as he started to wonder how he could have been hit by a car and walk away uninjured, the door opened. In walked the leader of The Circle – Salacious Cain. Camper always wondered if he got his name from Star Wars or the Satanic Bible. He chuckled.

"Something funny?"

"No, no Salacious. Nothing at all."

Salacious Cain wore a long black robe and a circular medallion around his neck. His hair was slicked back and he wore far too many rings. He looked like he belonged in an eighties heavy metal video or perhaps as an extra in the movie *The Gate*.

"I see nothing funny about your present situation Camper."

"Of course not. You're right." Camper swallowed his giggling and tried to concentrate on the fact that he was still a prisoner, no matter how funny their leader looked.

"Camper King, aka the man with the hole in his head. How long have you been fighting the Great One? Ten years, fifteen?"

Camper tried to remember, but of course he couldn't. There were reasons. They had told him. The things he would see and do would drive a normal man crazy. That's why they took his memories. So he could keep doing those things. Every now and again something would slip by, nowadays more than usual, but those memories were too disjointed to cause anything other than the headaches. A few pills would knock them out in no time.

"Word on the street is that you're losing it King."

Salacious Cain: the only Satanist ever to use the expression *word on the street*. Camper chuckled again, but only on the inside.

"No Salacious. I haven't lost anything. If I do I'll be sure to give you a call."

"Your most recent job, I hear a civilian got killed. That's a shame. Little girl too. Now normally I wouldn't really care, but we're getting some of the heat for this and that's just not right."

Salacious always talked too much. Camper *did* remember that. He bent down slowly, as if still listening, and tucked a finger into his boot. Ah. Still there. Slowly and casually, as Satan's number one fan turned to sermonize to the empty room, Camper took the piece of yellow chalk in his finger and drew a small line across the curve of the circle.

"...and that is why *this* time you won't be going anywhere."

Salacious turned. Camper was standing up, smiling and tossing his chalk in the air.

"What was that? I'm sorry. I wasn't listening."

Salacious' eyes widened.

"What are you doing up?"

"Punching."

Camper let fly with a left hook and a right uppercut that would have made Ali proud. Salacious fell to the ground like a wet laundry bag. Out for the count. That felt good. And he'd enjoy remembering it too. Now he just had to get out of there. Shouldn't be too hard. The Circle was mostly all talk, a few tricks and zero muscle. It seemed the *great one* just thought they were too pathetic to deal with.

Camper opened the door, now dressed in Salacious' robes, and checked for guards. (Salacious had been wearing ripped jeans and an Alice Cooper tour T-shirt underneath. Camper would have considered taking the shirt if it had been from a better tour). Nobody in the hallway. So far so good. He slowly made his way through the compound, stopping once or twice to be saluted by young Satanists. He walked the dirt road outside for about fifteen minutes and came out in the city's industrial park. Luckily a cab was just passing by. Divine intervention? He chuckled to himself.

"Where to?"

"St. Patrick's Church."

The cabby looked over his costume.

"You serious?"

Camper nodded and took off the robe as they approached the church. He slid the medallion into his pocket as a memento and chucked the robe in a garbage bin on the curb.

3

St. Pat's was a small church in the heart of downtown. There was nothing particularly special about it, but when Camper became a priest it was his parish. And it was here that he got the call. The phone call. From the Vatican. Father Sal was the priest here now and the only physical connection that Camper had with his bosses in Rome. Sal was his religious M.

Father Sal Detore had a kind face, with patches of white hair at his temples. He looked tired today, especially in his eyes. Camper wondered, and not for the first time, what other responsibilities the old priest had.

"It's good to see you Camper. How have you been?"

"I've been better Sal. Things are pretty messed up."

"I've been reading the papers."

Father Sal led Camper to the back of the church, past the altar and into his office.

"Coffee?"

"Got anything carbonated?"

"I'm afraid not."

"Coffee's fine."

Sal put the coffee pot on. "We're all very worried about

you. This last business. Not very good."

"I wish I could say that everything was fine. But you know that I can't. I don't know what happened. She might have been a demon herself."

He remembered for a moment his vision from that night. The little girl holding his hand. The patterns in the stars. No. She was real. Real and innocent. He was sure of it.

"Maybe you should take some time off."

"Maybe you should let me look at the files."

Father Sal's expression changed. The coffee started percolating.

"You know that's something I can't do."

"Why not? I should be allowed to see them. More than anyone."

"The Vatican thought it best that given the special circumstances-"

"The memory loss."

"Yes. Given your memory loss it would be best not to show you the files of your cases. Looking at them may trigger your memory. And that's something that we want to avoid. Your memory Camper-"

"Would lead to madness. Or so they say."

Camper slumped in his chair and realized he hadn't eaten since he had been taken prisoner that night.

"Camper. No one wants you to go mad. The things you have seen. It's the only way for you to remain pure and untainted. I'm not even allowed to look at your reports myself for fear of spiritual contamination. Not that I haven't been tempted. "

"I'm not that pure Sal. And neither are you for that

matter."

"No. I don't suppose either of us is, but would you really like to wake up screaming every night? Or seeing things floating in front of your eyes?"

"Spots?"

"Camper. This is the choice you made. After your first assignment you were given the choice."

Camper remembered. He remembered the feelings anyway. Sometimes he even remembered the taste of the solution the old priest first gave him to *adjust* his memory. It made his skin crawl.

"A little girl died two nights ago Sal."

"And who's to say that little girl wasn't the Devil Incarnate? You don't remember any of it. It's entirely possible. I'd say it's even more than possible. You've been doing good work here Camper."

Camper shrugged. "I guess you're right. I've been at this a long time Sal. Maybe I'm just getting touchy in my old age."

"It's much more likely. Drink your coffee."

For a moment Camper stared at the drink in his hand. Was this how it was done? Some powders in his coffee? A syringe in his arm as he nodded off? He shook his head and took a big gulp, burning his tongue.

When Camper finally found himself at home he couldn't sleep. Even after a big feed of chicken. And chicken usually did the trick. There was an itch in the back of his skull. A little itch that was telling him that no, things weren't right. Things weren't right at all. He got up out of bed, put on some clothes, grabbed a hammer out of the cupboard and headed out the door. Fifteen minutes later he was bashing the lock on the back door of St. Patrick's Church. The lock came away easy. And before he knew it he was in the basement. How could Sal keep him in the dark? Surely the reports themselves weren't bad enough to make a man go mad?

"Now, where the hell is it?"

When his eyes adjusted to the dark he found a door, painted to match the wall. Leave it to the Vatican. As he went to open it, the light switched on.

"I thought you'd come back."

It was Father Sal. Holding a Louisville Slugger. It looked like he knew what to do with it too.

"Is that for me?"

"No. But there was the off-chance it could have been someone else. You never know. We're kind of in a dangerous business."

They stood there for a moment. Camper was caught red handed and he looked it.

"The door is locked by the way."

"I figured that."

Camper waved his hammer. Sal shook his head and reached into his pocket, taking out a key.

"Just let me know when you're finished," he smiled, and tossed the key to Camper. "And you're paying for the lock on the back door."

Camper caught the key and smiled back.

"You can take it out of my paycheck."

It was about time.

Inside was the mother load. Stacks of filing cabinets and rows of glass cases filled with artifacts. It looked like something you'd find in the basement of an old museum.

The air was musty and old, but the place had seen regular use. Just inside the door was a simple wooden table, with stacks of paper, files, folders and a cup full of pens. He didn't need to be a detective to tell him that was where he filled out his reports but it was the filing cabinets and the glass cases that he was more interested in. He knew he'd been at this a while, but he hadn't realized just how busy he'd been or just how rotten The Dot had become.

The cabinets were labeled according to date and it was easy enough to find the most recent file. The one he wanted wasn't very thick, only a few pages. Vampires trying to summon a demon. Well that explained the garlic and holy water, but no mention of a little girl. What did that mean? That she wasn't there? That he wasn't responsible? Or did he leave it out on purpose? If only he could remember. Some demons required a sacrifice. That might explain it, but if that was true he would have written it in the report. This was turning into a dead end. A concrete wall of a dead end. Putting the file down, he glanced toward the rows of other cabinets. Well, might as well.

It seemed Camper King had fought and defeated just about every supernatural horror in existence and many of them multiple times. Even a few doozies with names Lovecraft would have had trouble pronouncing. No wonder they made him forget everything that had happened. This was the stuff of nightmares. The real, dirty and slimy deal. The descriptions alone were enough to make him shiver. But there was something that didn't add up. Occasionally Camper came across a file with a page or two missing. And sometimes a folder that was completely empty. Sloppy filing? An error in numbering? Or excluded on purpose just like the little girl? Maybe there were things in his other cases that shouldn't have happened and that he never became aware of. The concrete wall was turning into a tunnel. And he wasn't sure that he wanted to crawl down it.

He put the first file into his coat and started back toward the door. As he was leaving his eyes fell across the glass cabinets. There were bits of bone, carved and engraved with ritual markings, pieces of clothing made of a material he had never seen before, rocks and gems labeled *volatile,* books written in ancient languages, a few weapons, ceremonial daggers and even a silver plated six shooter. His mouth curled into a smile.

"Now why would they be keeping this from me?" he said to himself as he lifted the glass.

The gun was a piece of work: Silver plated, carved with intricate filigree with a walnut handle. It wasn't just a piece of work, it as a piece of art. There was an inscription along the barrel that read *Acerbus et ingens.* Fierce and mighty. He liked that. There was even a leather pouch full of shells to go with it. Camper slipped the shooter into the back of his jeans and the pouch into his coat pocket.

"Find what you were looking for?" Father Sal's voice came out of the darkness of the other room. A light switched on. Camper quietly replaced the glass case and closed the door.

"Not exactly."

"I thought that might happen."

"But it doesn't mean I'm going to stop looking."

Father Sal nodded.

"A little girl died Sal."

"I know, son. I know. Come on up to the kitchen, I managed to wrangle a Root Beer for you."

Camper smiled and pulled his coat securely. He had a file in his pocket and a gun in his pants. Both stolen. And now he had to have a Root Beer with the parish priest. Not good.

"I'm sorry your search went poorly, Camper."

Father Sal had retrieved a can from the fridge and was getting a glass from the cupboard.

"Sometimes you just have to take things on faith. You have to believe that what you do, no matter how terrible sometimes, is the right thing to do. *Seek not to understand that you may believe, but believe that you may understand.*"

"I don't think it's a crisis of faith, Sal. It's a gut feeling. I don't remember most of what I do so I depend on two things: my training and my gut. And my gut is telling me that something went wrong and I need to know why."

Father Sal poured his drink and a long sigh escaped from his mouth.

"You just don't know when to quit do you?"

"Sorry?"

Suddenly Father Sal turned, launching the glass of Root Beer at Camper. Camper got his arm up just in time to block the glass before Sal jumped on him, reaching for his throat.

"You should have let sleeping dogs lie, King," he said in a voice that wasn't his own. "Now you're gonna have to pay for it."

Father Sal, a frail man of 65, suddenly seemed much stronger and Camper had trouble getting him away from his neck. As they struggled the chair underneath Camper gave way and they ended up on the floor, slipping in the Root Beer. Camper finally managed to wriggle away long enough to get out his gun. When he pointed it, Sal backed away.

"Who are you? Where's Sal?"

Everything was wrong here and Camper needed answers. His heart was beating so hard he thought it might pop out of his chest.

"I am one of the faithful, King. Sal's been gone for years or didn't you know? You've been good to us, but your usefulness is at an end."

Suddenly he launched himself at Camper and, acting on instinct alone, Camper pulled the trigger. Lucky there were bullets already in the thing. Probably silver bullets. And blessed. Acerbus et ingens indeed. The thing formally known as Father Sal Detore fell to the kitchen floor, writhing in pain.

"You fucking asshole! Do you know how much this hurts?!"

Camper fired again, putting a hole through the imposter's shoulder.

"No. Why don't you tell me?"

"Get stuffed." The creature inside Father Sal started to laugh.

"Tell me everything."

"I'm not going to tell you shit."

Camper raised his gun. Of course he wouldn't and would he even believe him if he did? Probably not. He fired three more shots until he was sure the thing's mortal host was gone. Poor Sal. Aside from Convenience Store Phil, Sal was the closet thing Camper had to a real friend.

Or at least someone that he saw on a regular basis. He wondered how long it had been since they had actually spoken to each other. He quickly drew a series of symbols around the body and, rooting in the cupboard, sprinkled salt on the floor around him. He had done this hundreds of times before; a little ritual that prevented the body from coming back from the dead. It was the ritual that had started the whole "Pentagram Killer" business. Camper hated it, but there wasn't much he could do. Things were already going to hell and in his line of work that was very bad indeed.

When Camper got home he emptied his pockets. Aside from his most recent case file and the gun, he had grabbed an engraved bone, a ritual knife, a few of the volatile gems and a couple of other files before leaving. He had also locked the archive and pushed a small cabinet in front of the disguised door, wiped his prints from the scene and called in an anonymous tip from a nearby pay phone. He could have covered his tracks more thoroughly, but he hadn't brought the necessary materials.

"Sal. How could you have let them inside you?"

He didn't understand it. The old priest shouldn't have been that susceptible to possession. There were rites and rituals protecting him, weren't there? It shouldn't have happened.

The television was no comfort. His favorite channel was playing The Exorcist. Great.

"We apologize for the interruption in programming. Police report that the Pentagram Killer has struck again. A priest at St. Patrick's Church was found dead tonight in what has been described as a cold blooded shooting. Ritual markings and salt

were found around the body. A possible witness to the crime has come forward and police are expecting to release a sketch of the killer tomorrow. We'll bring you more on this as information comes in."

Camper cringed. Of course. The taxi driver.

4

"No man, the nose should be smaller than that. Yeah. That's alright."

Jimmy the cabby sat in a little room in the cop shop with Frenchie the sketch artist. His name wasn't really Frenchie, but he was the only cop on the force that spoke French and had been to France so Frenchie it was.

"Is this okay for the eyebrows?"

"Man. You've got 'em with a uni-brow. Guy didn't have a uni-brow."

"Ok." Frenchie took out his eraser. Usually he could get a sketch out of a witness fairly quickly, but it was late and he was tired. And the witness was tired too.

"How's that sketch going?"

Detective Gamby wasn't. Which was just annoying. Did she ever sleep?

Frenchie held his sketchpad up for Gamby's approval.

"Almost there. Good. Keep it up. I want that sketch on every TV channel tomorrow and in every newspaper. I want to hear *stop the presses* ringing out across the city."

Gamby had a flair for the dramatic.

"Man you don't have the ears right. And his hair should be different."

Frenchie was starting to wonder if Jimmy the cabby had actually seen this guy, but then he had the robe and that was something. More than something.

Detective Gamby sat at her desk. She was one of those cops with just enough seniority to get a relatively new computer, but not enough to have a desk near a window. Newspaper clippings and crime scene photos were spread out in front of her. Drawings of ritual markings were held down with a happy face coffee mug. And in five years the biggest piece of evidence they had ever gotten: a robe worn by the killer. She picked it up and looked it over. Simple cotton, black with a hood. Almost nothing special about it. Nothing that would indicate where it was made and by who. In fact it was so simple it could have been a Halloween costume. So Jimmy the cabby picks up a guy wearing this robe and a medallion (she wishes she had *that*) and drops him off at St. Patrick's Church where a priest is killed in cold blood that night, his body surrounded with symbols and markings matching the M.O. of the Pentagram Killer. Cut and dry. Once that sketch was out it would just be a matter of time.

"How's that sketch doing?"

Frenchie groaned. And so did Jimmy the cabby.

5

Frenchie and Jimmy weren't the only ones who were tired. Camper King tossed and turned all night. Almost as if he knew what was happening in the cop shop. He had spent the night going over some of the files he had stolen from the Church. Really nasty stuff. His previous case featured a family of vampires. If they could be called a *family*. Seems they were traveling from town to town, renting rooms and killing all their neighbors. Camper had posed as a neighbor to root them out but it turned out the vampires were servants of a demon and had been bringing sacrifices to it. And that's when things got nastier.

Camper decided to get up for some water. It was hot that night. Hotter than it should have been. He got a glass from the cupboard and as he turned the tap a memory flashed in his brain. A memory so strong that he dropped his cup. It shattered across the floor brilliantly. Camper didn't notice. His mind's eye was working overtime.

Please don't kill us mister.

I'm sorry but there's no other way.

I don't want to die.

Don't worry it'll only hurt for a second.

Camper raised his gun at the little boy in front of him. He was covered in strange tattoos and standing inside a crudely drawn hexagram on the floor. They were in an old wooden house. Abandoned and boarded up. The wind passed through the boards and made it feel like they were outside, not in. He fired three shots and the boy fell to the floor.

Camper held his head and took a step back, cutting himself on the glass. He let out a groan and sat at the kitchen table to pick it out of his foot. It was bloody and painful, but superficial. He wasn't worried about it. But a memory had gotten back in and that *did* worry him. He was being used, he knew that. But being used for what? And by who? Those were the questions he needed answered. He only hoped his memories would come back before the police got him.

6

"How ya doing, Phil?"

Camper had had the worst night of sleep in his life. All he wanted was his Cherry Coke and maybe someone to whack him on the head with a hammer.

"I guess you haven't seen the news today?"

"Huh?" Camper leaned over the counter to have a look at Phil's little black and white TV.

"What you are seeing right now is a composite sketch of the Pentagram Killer, put together last night with the assistance of an eye witness near the scene of the brutal killing of Father Sal Detore. If you have seen this man please contact the police immediately. Do not approach him. He is considered-"

Phil switched the TV off.

"I know you didn't."

"Thanks Phil."

"They get those sketches messed up easy."

Camper nodded and headed to the cooler for his Cherry Coke. He passed by the newspaper rack. He was on the front page. As he looked up a women and her son were staring at him. He smiled politely and they dropped everything and left the store. Great. Things were about to get real hairy. He could feel it in his bones.

7

Somewhere else in the city, far away from Phil's American Style Convenience, something else was waking up late. Something not human. With ears that weren't really ears it heard its master's voice calling. Its orders were simple. Just three words. Kill Camper King. With these words firmly locked in its brain, the thing that was neither dog nor wolf crawled out of its hole in the wall of an abandoned gas station and sniffed the air. Quickly picking up the scent it started to run. Kill Camper King. That was exactly what it was going to do.

8

American Style Phil was replenishing his stock of Cheezies when he heard the sirens. He looked out the window and down the road. Sure enough. Six cars with lights blaring and sirens wailing were pulling in around Camper's little house. He had never actually been to Camper's house, but he had some ideas about what it must be like inside. Guess he'd never have a chance to now. Cops were pouring out of the cars, guns out and ducked behind their open doors. A woman with a megaphone took front and center.

"Camper King! Come out with your hands up! We have you surrounded!"

Poor Camper.

"Phil!"

He was a decent guy.

"Phil!"

Phil turned around. He had forgotten that Camper was still in the store. He had been hiding behind a rack of disposable cameras.

"What are you doing here? The police have your house surrounded!"

"Doesn't matter. You got a basement in this place? Or a cellar or backroom?"

Phil hesitated. Harboring a wanted man wouldn't look good for business that was for sure. But Camper had saved his life. Probably. What the hell.

"The brown door in the back."

"You're a lifesaver."

Phil went back to watching the cops while Camper made for the back door. Turns out it was nothing more than a glorified broom closet. But at least there was room to sit. Damn. He should have bought some snacks first and maybe Phil's little TV.

"We know you're in there! Come out with your hands up!"

Gamby turned to a cop next to her, a muscle bound and mustached rookie named Rick. "Do we even know if he's in there?"

Rick shrugged. "According to his neighbors he doesn't get up til noon. He goes to the store and comes back home. And he's there til the evening. Same routine every day."

Gamby already knew this, but she needed to hear it out loud. She had conscripted a lot of manpower for the operation and couldn't go back empty handed. There was too much at stake.

"Ok. Rick, spread the word, we're going in."

"Yes Ma'am."

Rick made his way from car to car. He was efficient; she could say that much for him. Policemen started breaking off in pairs, slowly approaching the house from the side and back. A few stayed with the cars in front both for show and in case he made a run for it. Gamby went for the back door.

"On three," she said, locking eyes with the cops near her. "One. Two. Three!"

The back door wasn't locked and Gamby and her officers went pouring through it. Within minutes they had every inch of the house covered and not a sign of Camper King.

She ended up sending most of the cops back to headquarters, with a car parked out front in case he came back. Although there was little chance of that. He probably took off as soon as he saw his picture in the paper. Damn it. Still, at least they had his name. And his house. There had to be something there. She started looking around. The place looked like something out of a catalogue. Everything in its own little place. Except the bedroom, which looked like it belonged to a teenager. In the kitchen trash she found a piece of paper towel covered in blood and bits of glass.

"Rick."

Rick was still in the house. Probably his first time at a crime scene and he had no intention of going back to file.

"Call the lab. They should really have some of their boys up here going over the place."

Rick disappeared out the back.

The fridge was pretty much empty aside from a few cans of Cherry Coke and an opened microwave dinner covered in plastic wrap. Thank God. She was expecting body parts. The cupboards turned up the same; a haven for cup noodles. Something wasn't right. If this guy was a serial killer shouldn't his house be just a little bit creepier? A basement satanic altar? Bulletin board of newspaper clippings? Maybe it was all a front. She wasn't sure. That's when she found the file. It was just sitting on the kitchen table next to a newspaper. And when she started reading she realized things were a lot more complicated than anyone had suspected. She tucked the file inside her coat when the lab boys showed up. No one was seeing it. Not if she could help it.

9

Phil turned away from the window. Cop cars were driving away and things were starting to calm down a bit. He grabbed a can of Cherry Coke and a bag of chips and walked to the back.

"Camper? Looks like most of them are gone. You hungry?"

Camper opened the door and Phil dropped the can. Rick the rookie had just walked into the store for a quick snack. He had his gun out and was trembling.

"It's okay officer. This guy was only helping me because I threatened him. It's okay. I'm getting up now."

"Slowly!"

"Yup. Nice and slow. Phil you better back up there in case the young man's finger slips."

Phil obliged. Rick eyed him warily.

"See. No trouble at all."

Camper walked out of the broom closet with his hands in the air. His legs had fallen asleep and it was a job to stay upright, but with a gun pointed his way he made sure not to fall. Rick fumbled with the talkie on his shoulder. He didn't see the thing coming toward the window. No one did. Until it was too late.

10

Gamby's talkie sparked to life. The voices that came from it were fragmented and desperate.

Oh man what is that? ..arghhhh! ..Get down! get down! ..In nomine patri ..Holy shit! ..Camper! ..et filia ..sancti ..Camper!

And then the radio went dead. She recognized Rick's voice. She knew that. Where had he gone? Couldn't be far since he had just been there. She took out her gun and ran out the front door. Panic started to set in. It was a feeling she hadn't felt since she was as rookie. She didn't like not being in control. Closing her eyes she took a deep breath and let the training take over. The patrol car was gone. She quickly scanned the area. No one nearby. And then she caught a glimpse of the store down the street. She hot footed it down there as fast as she could, but by the time she arrived, it was all over.

11

Camper King wiped the blood from his sleeve. Good thing he had had that bone in his pocket. Although had he known it was volatile he would have probably left it at home. In a blast-proof safe. Phil's American Style Convenience looked like it had been hit by a hurricane. The front window was smashed in, shelves were knocked over and food was everywhere. The register was lodged in a wall and an unusual amount of the stores products had found their way out into the parking lot. Especially Cheesies. The pavement was coloured with patches of orange. Lying amongst the rubble was a hell hound. Big one too. Neither wolf nor dog. That was the traditional description, but the old books always left out the details: an almost human face, the lack of visible ears, spoon shaped nose, claws like forks, eyes like cold dishes and fangs as long as a man's hand. Not to mention their insatiable appetite for destruction. Hell hounds were treasured as pets. Play things for the damned and they were very rarely released into the human world. When they were it was always for a purpose. This one was looking for Camper. He knew it. He knew it in his mostly exploded bone.

"Is everyone okay?"

Phil called out from behind the counter in a foreign language Camper didn't recognize. And there were very few he didn't know. The cop was in pretty hard shape, but he'd live. Thank God for small miracles. And with the huge corpse of a hell hound lying across aisles one and two there was no way they could pin this one on him. The proof was in the pudding and the pudding was four hundred pounds.

"Everybody freeze! Hands in the air! What the hell is that?!"

Another cop. Great. Camper decided to be graceful.

"Officer. If you would allow me to explain-"

"You stay exactly where you are. You move a hair on your arm and I fire. You understand?"

"Perfectly."

Gun still raised the young cop, detective most likely, made her careful way around the body of the beast and checked on the other cop.

"He's still breathing officer. Just needs some medical attention."

"What did I just say? A hair…"

Gamby almost considered firing. She finally had the serial killer in her sights, but then there was the coyote or bear maybe or whatever it was. What was it doing there? And the file she had found back at the house. None of it made any sense. She radioed for back-up and ordered a medic for Rick. Poor Rick. He was a bit dumb, but he had a good heart.

"What about my store?"

She raised her gun toward the counter. Didn't know

there was a civilian there. This was not a good time to be sloppy. She took a deep one. A small man with a balding head popped up where the register should have been. He was waving a wet nap like a flag.

"Are you injured sir?"

"No. I don't think so. Camper told me to stay put behind here and that's exactly what I did."

She gave the killer a look. What was he playing at?

"What about my store?"

"I'm sure your insurance will cover it, sir."

"No. They'll call it an act of God. Believe me I know. I know how those people work."

"This wasn't an act of God." Camper was eyeing the hell hound. "Quite the opposite."

All eyes turned to the creature, which was already starting to decompose and rapidly too. Maggots had appeared in its dark fur and its eyes had liquefied. It made Gamby sick to look at it. Not to mention the smell. Like three week old fast food garbage. She barely suppressed the urge to urge.

"What's this bear doing here?"

Camper whistled low.

"If you think that's a bear, then you need more Discovery Channel in your diet."

"Then what is it?"

A voice came from where the door used to be.

"Canus inferni. A hound of hell. "

It was Salacious Cain, decked out in full Satanic regalia. He lifted his robe slightly before entering the doorway and he had the slickest smile on his face as he did. Gamby didn't know where to point her gun. The world was tumbling upside down. Salacious made his way across the rubble. He was oily, moving across the dented tin cans and broken boxes of pasta like a snake. If a snake could walk.

"No need for arms, Officer."

"I'll make that decision." She took a look back at Camper. Camper returned it with the universal look for *this guy's an asshole.* She had seen that look enough on the force to know what it meant.

Salacious seemed to be enjoying the whole affair, oblivious to both the gun and the cop holding it.

"Looks like someone finally got your scent Camper. It's about time too."

"You don't know the half of it Salacious."

The cop chuckled despite herself.

Salacious rolled up his sleeves, which Camper knew was a sign that he was about to start speechifying. It would be long and boring. He knew it. Well why not? Once again Camper was stuck with nothing to do but listen. Thankfully, three things happened all at once to prevent it.

Sirens blared outside as the cop's backup and an emergency van finally showed. The body of the hell hound burst into flames for no apparent reason and started to melt through the floor, throwing the cop off balance. And to top it off a can of peas came flying through the air from Phil's direction, nailing the cult leader in the face. Betcha that hurt. Phil was smiling when Camper looked over at him. Retrieving his charred bone from the floor, bite marks and all, Camper took it as an opportunity to try the back door. Phil gave him a wave as Gamby made it to her feet. The guy in the robe was out cold. The store owner was smiling. The creature was almost completely melted away. And Camper was gone! She jumped toward the back door but he was nowhere to be found. She clicked on her radio.

"This is Gamby. Suspect has fled on foot out the back door of Phil's Convenience. I want this whole road blocked."

More police arrived, stumbling over the wreckage and two EMTs took Rick out on a stretcher. He was mumbling as they took him away.

"Camper saved us all…"

Gamby holstered her weapon. It didn't matter. She wasn't going to let him get away.

12

There wasn't much Camper could do when he took off but head back home. It looked like all the cops were gone, but that would change within a few minutes. Not a lot of time. He quickly grabbed a change of clothes (his own were covered in dead hell hound) and his silver gun. The cops hadn't found his stash yet, though he wasn't surprised. His bedroom was a state. Lucky he could even find pants in there. He did manage to find his sunglasses though. Small joys.

Camper didn't have many friends. His line of work left little room for a social life, but he didn't mind it. Friends would just complicate things. He didn't even have a computer let alone a facebook account. Now that the shit had actually hit the fan there were very few places he could go for sanctuary.

13

"Mom?"

The little apartment in the old age complex smelled like cheese. She loved the stuff. There were always strange cheeses in the house when he was a kid. She would get them delivered twice a week and he always tried to avoid the inevitable taste testing. It had taken him an hour and three buses to get there. He hoped it was worth it. His head felt like it was full of cotton balls and he just didn't know what else to do.

"Is that my little dickie?"

A little old lady with blue hair and a matching blue nightgown came out of the kitchen. Camper breathed a sigh of relief and closed the front door, locking it behind him.

"It's me Mom. How are you doing?"

"Let me look at you."

She grabbed his hand and led him to a plastic covered couch. Sitting next to him she reached her hands upwards to touch his face.

"You look worried."

Mrs. King had been blind since the age of four, but it

hadn't stopped her from doing anything. She was now a very spry eighty-eight.

"Just work stuff Mom."

"You shouldn't let work get you all worried like that. Your father, God rest his soul, never brought his work home, but I suppose it's different for you."

Camper shrugged.

"How's your parish?"

"Fine Mom. It's fine."

He hadn't told her about his *transfer,* but then again who would believe him? Yes Mom, I've been transferred from my post as parish priest by an office of the Vatican that isn't supposed to exist. I spend my days and nights battling the forces of darkness. The weekly allowance isn't bad, but the side effects are a killer. Yeah. Sure she'd like to hear that.

"Everything will work out. Don't you worry about it. Would you like a cookie?"

Camper smiled for the first time in days. Actually he almost cried. Of course he would like a cookie. It might not solve all his problems, but it couldn't hurt. And chocolate chip was his favourite.

Mrs. King got up to get the cookie tin from the kitchen. The sun was coming out. It streaked through the living room window and fell across the pictures all over the wall. His mom might not have been able to see, but she still made sure she had pictures of all her relations on the wall. It was just then that another memory started sneaking back into his mind. It felt like someone was slowly pushing an icicle into his brain.

He was standing in a warehouse. There were men in

robes standing around the body of a young woman. The were chanting but he couldn't make out the words. Someone near her raised a dagger. Camper raised his gun and started shooting. Within fifteen seconds everyone in a robe was on the ground. The woman had been cut by the dagger before he could fell the leader.

"You have to kill me."

"I'm not going to do that."

"If you don't. It will come through"

Camper looked into her eyes. They were darkening over. She was changing into something.

"Please."

Her teeth were changing. Rapidly getting longer and sharper.

He raised his gun. And lowered it. He was too weak for this.

"You have to do it! Do it now! Before it's too late!"

She started screaming. Camper closed his eyes, fired three shots and let the silver gun hang at his side. Never again, he promised himself. He would always get there on time.

"Now how about that cookie?"

Ma King had returned with her tin of cookies. Camper took time for a big chocolate chip. It was just soft enough. She always made them just like that and as the taste filled his mouth he could feel the bad memories slipping away.

"Mom why don't you have a little lie down? I've got to be going soon anyway."

He led her to the bedroom and as he closed the door he heard her say "You were always my little special boy. You always did the right thing."

Camper wasn't sure anymore. Minutes later he was in

her bathroom, shaving his head with his Dad's old razor. With his picture up all over town, he had to do something. Just before leaving he clicked on the TV to see if there was anything about the store on the news channel.

"According to witnesses at the scene an ambulance also took away a man dressed in a black robe. An officer, who refused to be identified, has told us they believe this man to be the Pentagram Killer and is assuring residents that their city is safe."

Camper laughed to himself. Thank God. Then he found himself wondering how long it would take for Salacious to wake up and point the finger where it belonged.

14

"Yeah, that looks kinda like him"

Gamby was holding a polaroid of Salacious, taken in the hospital, in front of Jimmy the cab driver, who seemed to have changed his mind about the face of the killer.

"Are you sure?"

"Pretty sure."

Gamby didn't understand it. Everything seemed to point to King. But the statements made by Phil and Rick didn't make sense. Camper was some sort of convenience store superhero? Couldn't be. But then there was the bear or whatever it was decomposing before her eyes; gone before any of the other officers had arrived. And there was the file sitting at the bottom of her desk. A file that made no sense whatsoever but seemed to collaborate the statements made by Phil and Rick. It was just too wild an idea to consider. Maybe when the guy named Salacious woke up she'd get some answers.

The lab hadn't come up with anything in Camper's house. The blood on the glass matched blood found on a razor in the bathroom and traces were found on the kitchen floor. Probably just an accident. His parents were both listed as deceased and he had no employment record. For all intents and purposes he was a ghost. And she desperately wanted to get that ghost into an interrogation room.

15

Salacious opened his eyes. His head was fuzzy and his eyes as well. There were things coming out of his nose. Tubes he thought. Wires? No. Tubes for sure. He tried lifting his arm. No good. He was too weak to move. What happened? Camper King. Something about Camper King. And there was a cop wasn't there? And something had hit him in the head. He blinked. Things were becoming a bit clearer now, but he felt so weak. He shouldn't be this weak from a little bang on the head. He tried looking around. He was alone in a white room. There was a machine next to him, beeping steadily perhaps to remind him that he was still alive. The window curtains were closed. He looked toward the door. There was a shape in the window. It looked policeman shaped. Was he being guarded or protected? Well, better to find out. He gathered his strength to call out and just as he opened his mouth to do so a hand came out of nowhere and covered it. His eyes bulged out in shock. It was cold, very cold.

"If you know what's good for you, you won't make a sound."

The voice was hushed and rapid. He decided to oblige

it. The hand moved away from his mouth and Salacious kept looking forward.

"We want Camper King back. We're losing him. Do you understand what I mean?"

Salacious had no idea, but he nodded anyway.

"We want things to be the way they used to be. That rat Gamby has been trying to ruin all of it for years."

He wanted to ask what and thought better of it. Whoever this was had gotten into the room without the guard noticing. Hell, he hadn't even *been* there a moment ago.

"Kill Vanessa Gamby, do you understand?"

He didn't, not really, but again he nodded. He was still feeling so fuzzy.

"Kill her for the Great One."

His eyes bulged again. The Great One? But didn't they just try to kill King? He remembered seeing the corpse of the hell hound. What made them change their mind? But he was a servant. He had to remind himself of that. And servants didn't ask questions. They went where they were wanted. And they killed when they were told. Or they suffered the consequences.

The voice was quiet now and Salacious risked turning his head to look. No one there. He suppressed a shiver. The window was closed and there was no other way into the room. Well, first things first. He had to get out of bed, find some pants and get past the guard. No sweat.

16

Camper had been wandering the street all day. His disguise seemed to be working. No one really gave him a second look. In fact, people went out of their way to avoid him. He had taken an old brown coat from his mother's place that used to belong to his father. It smelled like cigars and was long enough that it hid the gun in his pants. It also had deep pockets, perfect for what was left of his magic bone. The bone had come in handy once already and he wasn't taking any chances. He passed by a pharmacy. No need for Aspirin anymore. Since his memories had started coming back the headaches had stopped. It was just then that he realized he still remembered the fight with the hell hound. He still had the memory. Hadn't lost it yet. The memory loss was fading and he was returning to normal after all those years. He waved a hand in front of his eyes. No spots. That was good. Sal would be happy about that. For a moment he considered a regular life. No more supernatural encounters. No more killing. He could just settle down somewhere and relax. Quit the priesthood and maybe even get married. His attitude toward the church had certainly changed in the past little while. Then he caught his reflection in the pharmacy window. He was bald and his eyes were dark underneath. It looked like he hadn't slept in days. Someone you wouldn't want to meet in a dark alley, let alone marry. Armed and dangerous? The police had that much right.

Just as he was raising his arm for the number eight bus he felt a sharp pain in his head. Another memory was flooding in, but this one so quickly and fragmented that his brain couldn't catch up with it. It was like a box of jigsaw-puzzle pieces had been poured into his brain and he had no idea how to put them together. Or even what the picture on the box was supposed to look like. He needed to look at the files again. He needed answers. As crazy as it was, he had to go back to St. Pat's. And he had to do it soon.

17

When Vanessa Gamby arrived at St. Bartholomew's Hospital she was more than furious. She was insane. No one, not even the guard with the nasty and bleeding bump on his head, was safe from her wrath. How did it happen? No one knew. And with all the guards outside? Ridiculous. Someone was going to pay for this. Salacious Cain. He knew Camper. And he was wearing the same kind of robe that Camper had been wearing the night of the murder at St.Pat's. They were connected. It had even occurred to her that they might *both* be the Pentagram Killer. Collaborating with each other, or perhaps competing in some sick game. Everything she had read in the case file and every memory she had of the decomposing animal corpse disappeared from her mind. People were dead and these two men were connected to it or responsible for it. They were going to be found.

"Detective Gamby?"

"What is it?!"

The old doctor took a step backwards when Gamby yelled and then slowly raised an eyebrow.

"I'm sorry. It's been a long day. I'm sorry who are

you?"

"I'm Doctor Martin. I've been observing Jeremy for the past twenty four hours."

"Jeremy?"

"Jeremy Daniels. The young man with the head injury. You've had him guarded since he came in."

Of course. Salacious Cain. The EMTs had provided his wallet when they got him in. No known relatives however. Her angry was clouding her memory. She had to keep cool and under control. The case couldn't afford any more mistakes.

"Perhaps we could speak in my office?"

Dr. Martin led Gamby to a little room down the hall. It smelled like old coffee and cleaning detergent. A million thoughts were running through her head and none of them good. She was sure the doctor was going to tell her Salacious had abnormalities in his brain and was a danger not just to the public but also to himself. That there was nothing they could do for him other than putting him in an institution.

He did no such thing.

"I've been following the case, Detective Gamby."

He sat back in his leather chair. Great. Another nut. She sighed. He wouldn't be the first one who had told her that he'd cracked the case. But there were plenty that they had kept out of the papers. Everyone assumed pentagrams and bloody knives. Not the case. In fact there were more Christian symbolism than pagan found at the crime scenes. And not always bodies. Sometimes just bits of clothing; scraps of evidence that so and so had existed and was now nowhere to be found. She settled into her chair and steeled herself. Here come the armchair deductions.

"Nothing about the case makes sense to me, Detective."

Here we go.

"Have you ever heard of the Society for the Recognition of Meta-states?"

Oh boy. Total nut job. And a doctor to boot. She didn't have time for this. She should be out there right now, scouring the streets with the rest of the force. The Society for what? Who knew.

"The Society for the Recognition of Meta-states."

Wait a second.

"Yes. I am able to read your mind. It's not something I do often and never without the permission of the person I am reading."

He leaned forward, interlocking his fingers and looked her straight in the eye.

"But I believe we have an interesting opportunity here, Detective. An opportunity for both us."

This had to be bullshit.

"No Detective. It's not."

She blinked and tried to empty her mind of everything.

"When I enter a Meta-State I am extending my maximum capabilities, both mental and physical. For some it is stronger in one more than the other. I happen to favour the mental amplification. For example…"

He motioned to a shelf on the opposite wall. Books started to move on their own, rearranging themselves on the shelf. Gamby should have fainted, but she was well beyond that. She just didn't give a shit anymore. Bigfoot could have walked in at that moment giving a piggyback to a grey alien and dragging the Loch Ness Monster on a leash behind them and she wouldn't have even given them a second look.

"Two of them are real. One isn't. Just thought you'd like to know."

Gamby looked at him and leaned forward. Between the creature at the convenience store and the strange file at King's house, she thought she'd seen enough crazy in the last two days. But what the hell. She had nothing to lose.

"What kind of opportunity?"

18

When Camper reached the church he found the back door unlocked and unguarded. Lucky, lucky. He slipped in through the door and into the kitchen, closing it behind him and jamming it with a chair. He didn't want any visitors. A faint chalk line still remained on the blood- and root beer-stained linoleum. It couldn't have been helped. It had to be that way and he was better off now. Better off dead than a puppet.

Camper started down the stairs to the basement when a memory hit him. Once again it was like a puzzle, making no sense, but this time it hit him so hard that he lost awareness of his feet underneath him. And the stairs too. The world toppled end over end and he found himself in the basement, flat on his stomach. He looked up at the stairs and the door above them. Could have been worse. Then he looked at his legs. It was worse. Much worse. His right leg had caught a piece of wood on the way down, probably had been sticking off of the railing. The pointy end had stuck into his lower leg and the force of the fall had driven it in deep. Camper wasn't even aware of the pain at first. He crawled a little ways until he found a box of old altar boy robes and ripped one in two. He gritted his teeth, yanked out the foot-long wooden splinter and started wrapping the cloth around it. That was going to need stitches. He was sure of it. And there was no way he could go to a hospital. Doing it himself was not a pleasant thought, but it was the only alternative. And in the meantime he still had to look at those files.

Hopping across the basement floor, Camper remembered he had dragged a filing cabinet in front of the archive door. With a tremendous effort he managed to shove it aside. Taking out the key to the place he unlocked the disguised door. Nothing had been disturbed inside since he had killed Sal- since he had killed the *demon* that had taken over Sal. Obviously the police hadn't found the room, or just hadn't searched the basement. He looked at the cabinets. The dusty old room looked more like an ancient wine cellar or catacomb and the cabinets looked entirely out of place. Clean and shiny, sitting side by side in perfect order, each drawer neatly labeled with the year. But where to start? That was a question. Well, at the beginning. Why not? He probably had all night anyway.

19

Eddie Tripper, one of the lowest ranking cultists in The Circle, was nervously tying his robe. Tonight he would be initiated into the Seventh Circle, his very first step toward greater power and the secrets of worshiping the Great One. Eddie came from a middle class home with middle class parents and middle class siblings. He didn't drive BMWs and Jags like most of the other members. His father wasn't a lawyer or a doctor and his mother had never been Miss Sunshine Patch '89 or some such nonsense. He wasn't there because he was bored. And he wasn't there because he was rebelling against his family. He truly believed. And he wanted the power that was promised. None of the other initiates believed like he did. They giggled and played pranks and drank beer. For them The Circle was more of a fraternity than a religious organization. That was why he was being promoted. Finally someone had recognized that he was different. That he was destined to advance.

The doors were opened and Eddie walked through them. He was in the Great Hall of The Circle. On the floor were drawn a series of large circles and within each circle, a number of chairs. The largest being the seventh. Inside this circle was the sixth. And then the fifth. And so on until the very center circle. The First Circle. And inside that circle, three chairs. The heads of the Order sat there. But today there was an empty seat. Salacious Cain was missing. Eddie took his seat outside the circles with the rest of the Unworthy. But not for long. Today he would move up to the next row of chairs and truly belong.

"We begin this council in the Great One's name."

One of the two men in the center circle had stood. His name was Malicious Black. The other was Voracious Sin. Everyone took their seats. A sea of black robes.

"Edward Tripper please step forward."

Eddie got up and made his way toward the aisle that led through all the circles. This was as close as he had ever been to the leaders. His hands were shaking and he was sweating down his back. The thick robe wasn't helping either. When he came to power that would be his first two orders of business: thinner robes and air conditioning.

Already aware and prepared for the ritual to take place, Eddie knelt in front of the three chairs and rolled up his wide sleeves. The next part was going to hurt, but he was ready for it. Pain was a part of the process. Only through pain could one learn how to worship the Great One.

Suddenly the doors to the hall burst open and Salacious Cain flew in. The whole assembly was on its feet and everyone started talking at once. No one had ever dared to interrupt one of their meetings. Well, no one since Camper King back in '91. Eddie had only heard rumours of the incident from some of the other

Unworthy. It wasn't something that the higher-ups liked to talk about. Salacious' eyes were bloodshot and his hair thrown in every direction. His face was dirty and pale white all at the same time. He looked every bit the part of a desert prophet, lacking only a sign that said *The End is Nigh!* Under his hospital robes every part of him was trembling.

He raised his arms in the air with tubes still attached and dangling.

"The Great One has spoken to me!"

There was a moment of complete silence and then the whole assembly started shouting. Voracious rapped a hammer against his chair. He looked over at Salacious. Oh how the mighty hath fallen. He wanted Salacious' center chair more than anything. He smiled on the inside. Now was the opportunity to grab it.

20

Vanessa Gamby rolled over in her bed. Her mind was reeling. Meta-States. Demons. Monsters. She'd been involved in the case of the Pentagram Killer on and off for almost ten years now and suddenly it was turning into a cheap eighties horror flick. Nothing seemed real anymore. A world had been revealed to her. Or part of a world. She wasn't sure what she believed, but the things that she had seen in Dr. Martin's office couldn't have been a trick. Books moving on their own. Mind reading. He had told her that he could help her capture King and Jeremy Daniels. And all he wanted in exchange was a chance to read King's mind. Why he'd want to do that she didn't know, but she needed to use every available tool she could get her hands on. The deal was made and the Doctor's fellow members in the Society for the Recognition of Meta-States were moving across the city, probably that very night, trying to find them. Something about it made her uneasy. She was a police officer and what were they? A gang? Vigilantes? But finding King and Daniels was more important than that. They had to be found before anyone else died. Suddenly she heard feedback and then applause. The bar across the street was just getting fired up. She had forgotten it was Friday night. And here she was in bed at eleven o'clock. Must be getting old. She put a pillow over her head to drown out the noise. It started to rain. The sound of the water hitting her window helped. At least a little.

21

Things had changed in The Circle. Salacious knew it. He knew it the moment he had burst into the Great Hall and made his announcement. He could see it in everyone's eyes. Even the Unworthy had looked down on him. They had become lazy, complacent and unable to see the wonder of their cause when it was staring them straight in the eye. Voracious had taken the center chair immediately. Salacious hadn't been surprised by that. What *did* surprise him was their leniency. He had been taken to a smaller office and given the chance to plead his case to the members of the first circle. They didn't listen. Salacious was exiled. Cast out and proclaimed a heretic. Not to mention a liability. They had been secretly worshiping for years, only doing those things that would go unnoticed, and now Salacious wanted them to kill a cop. And not just any cop: the detective leading the Pentagram Killer investigation. The Circle *wanted* Camper King to be caught. Why would the Great One want him protected? It didn't make sense. So without any ceremony, Salacious was shown the door. It wouldn't have been that way in his father's time. Blood would have been spilled.

Rites initiated. Loose ends tied up. And now Salacious was just Jeremy. Just Jeremy still in a hospital robe, soaked in the rain and alone in the street. Barefoot and abandoned. Maybe the voice he had heard wasn't real. Maybe it was all in his head, a mix of drugs and coma-dreams. *That* made sense. If it wasn't for the feeling inside him, that said it had happened.

"Get the fuck down! Now!"

The voice had come from an alleyway close by. Salacious didn't have any fear any more. He was a man with nothing to lose.

"What's going on down here?"

He spoke calmly. Almost too calmly. Like a forties mobster about to pull a hit. Down the alley was a man dressed in jeans and a black jacket. He had a gun pointed at the ground. On the ground there was a man and a woman. The man was on his knees with his wallet out. The woman was on her back. Her lip was bleeding.

"Who the hell are you?"

Salacious laughed. The guy with the gun was probably sixteen. About the same age that he had been when he had joined The Circle. Pathetic. Nothing mattered anymore. One way or the other. He sat down on the ground, singing to himself. The kid shrugged him off as another homeless lunatic and put his attention back on the couple. The man's hands were trembling as he handed over a wad of bills. Salacious moved his finger in the mud of the alley, drawing a circle with a ragged line through it. As he finished the line he pointed to the kid.

"Drop the gun."

He did so. A look of panic crossed his face. Salacious

liked it.

"Now run towards the wall."

The kid took a dash toward the facing brick wall of the alley and struck it head on. He went out cold and fell to the ground. Salacious moved his hand across the circle, wiping it clean. The man helped the woman get to her feet and then moved toward him. His eyes were thankful, but fearful as well.

"Thank you."

Salacious looked up at them and something clicked. Something deep inside him that he didn't know was there. A little piece that had gotten lost twenty years ago. That one remaining fragment of goodness. He had only gone down the alley because he was hurt, rejected, insulted and wanted to inflict some pain, but it all got turned around. Here he was. For the first time in his life, a hero. A soaked, beaten and possibly demented hero, but a hero nonetheless.

He smiled and started to laugh again. The rain poured down in buckets and the couple left the alley. He remained. Laughing in the rain. Laughing and free and insane.

22

Camper sat there in the secret room below St. Pat's Church, trying to put his mind back together. He felt a little like an archeologist, sitting in a dusty basement with hundreds of tiny pottery pieces, trying to put Humpty Dumpty back together again. The strangest thing about it all was recognizing his handwriting in the files, but not having any recollection of actually writing in them. For the first time Camper was recognizing the paradox. He had spent years fighting the forces of evil, but he was still kind of a rookie. He didn't have access to the lessons he would have learned from those experiences. He knew things of course. He trained, he read books, he dealt with more mundane sorts of evil, but close-encounters with the demonic were non-existent in his memory. And to top it all off he was being used; manipulated during those moments with the knowledge that no one would ever know. Until now. Since he had killed the demon inside Sal his memories were leaking back in. The answer to it all had to be in the files. That one pottery piece that would let all the others fall into place.

His leg was hurting real bad. His makeshift bandage

had turned a dark pink. His head felt dizzy and his eyes more blurry than usual. There were mounds of files left to sort through, but he realized he'd have to take care of the leg first. There was no getting around it. And that meant getting back upstairs.

23

It was no good. She wasn't going to sleep tonight. Not with the band playing across the street and her thoughts running a twenty-four hour marathon inside her head. Vanessa Gamby got up, put on some real clothes and left her apartment. It was cold outside. Cold and dark. One of those nights when the cold would creep into you no matter what you were wearing. The moon wasn't quite full and was half hidden behind sickly clouds. City clouds. Not the kind she grew up with in sleepy Shepherd's Grove. Her father had been a cop and so had her grandfather so it kind of ran in the family. She was the one to take it a step further, taking off to The Dot, but she had always been like that. If her friends were playing a game as kids, she'd be the one trying to set up a league. When her father asked her what she wanted to be when she grew up she told him a crime fighter, like Charlie's Angels, only without the hair and bell bottoms. She thought fighting evil was cut and dry. Bad guy breaks the law, arrest bad guy. But suddenly evil wasn't just something a bad person did. It was a physical thing itself. If people like Dr. Martin and his Society existed, then the opposite had to be true, hadn't it? She found herself cataloging every childhood closet monster she could think of and wondering how real they could be. Bad thoughts on a cold and dark night. She pulled her coat closer, feeling the bump under her arm where her pistol was holstered. Maybe she should have put in a request for silver bullets. She laughed at herself and shook her head. Maybe from now on garlic and holy water should be standard issue for cops on the beat.

Suddenly a car drove past and a bottle flew out the window, striking Gamby in the head. She could hear voices in the distance yelling *piggy! piggy! piggy!* For a moment they sounded like playground taunts. The kids making fun of her because her father was a cop, but that had happened in Shepherd's Grove year's ago. This was now. The car drove off and Gamby fell to her knees, clutching the back of her head. Her hair felt matted and sticky. A moment later there was an arm around her shoulder.

"Are you alright?"

The man's voice was calm and reassuring. She could barely keep her eyes open.

"I don't know. Probably a slight concussion."

"Maybe we should get you to the hospital."

She didn't want the hospital. It was nothing. Just an icepack that was all.

"No. No, as long as I can get home I'll be fine."

"Would you like me to get you a cab?"

The voice was so gentle. So assuring, but it sounded familiar too. She couldn't place it. For once she wanted someone to help her. She wanted to be the one being rescued. The one being protected and served.

"Could you bring me to my apartment? It's not far."

She held her hand out and he took it to help her up.

"My name is Vanessa."

She blinked, trying to clear her vision. There was something familiar.

"I'm Jeremy," he said. "And I'm supposed to kill you."

24

In his Meta-State Colt was the best at finding people. Everyone knew it. Some people in the Society called him the bloodhound, but never to his face. He didn't like the nickname. Didn't like being compared to a dog. There were powerful people in the group. Colt knew it. There was a girl in Kansas who had apparently lifted a house once. There was a guy in The Dot that could see through walls. Colt himself had seen a demonstration. And then there was the Doctor. He had abilities nobody even knew about. But put a name in Colt's brain and he could find that person blindfolded. He would just *know*. This time the name was Camper King.

All that he knew about him was that he was a priest. Or used to be one. And that he was armed and dangerous. Colt carried his own gun under his coat and a knife in his boot. He was pretty dangerous himself. He ran a hand through his shaggy blond hair. Above him, a neon sign blinked *Phil's American Style Convenience*. The door was locked with a *closed until further notice* sign taped to it. There must have been an accident. The front of the store had sheets of plywood nailed to cover a hole in the wall and the windows were also covered. Colt's brain was pounding. Camper King had been here. And often. He turned around and looked up the road. That made sense. His house was near by. Colt knew it instinctively. He also knew there was no way in hell Camper was there. He reached out with his mind. A bus. A dog. A silver gun. A razor. A blind woman. A church. The church made his brain pulse and light up like a Christmas tree. That was the place. And Colt didn't need any special abilities to know what church it was. It had been all over the headlines just a few days ago.

He took out his phone and called a cab. He always took cabs when he was looking for people. It helped keep him anonymous and it allowed him to put all his attention on the target. A few minutes later a car pulled up and he climbed in the back. The décor was a shrine to St. Mary, complete with pompoms and rosaries. Too perfect.

"Where to?"

"St. Patrick's Church. Fast as you can."

25

St. Patrick's Church had been built in the seventies. Thirty years before, a man named Charles Mugg had gotten rich in an unexpected oil boom just outside of town. Twenty wells and Mugg owned them all. Then in '63 a tornado ran through the city, dragging three trailers right through every one of Mugg's oil drills on their way to their eventual home in the middle of a Chicago suburb. Suffice to say Charles Mugg blamed the disaster on his lifestyle. Too much drink. Too many women. And not enough God. He devoted himself to the Church and when he passed in '72 of stomach cancer, he left everything to the local diocese with the expectation that a new church would be built. The thing was The Dot didn't need a new church. There were already plenty; almost an abnormal amount. But Mugg's will was very clear and the diocese was only going to get the money if they were willing to build a new church. So they did. And as a result of it being one of the most unused Churches on the continent of North America, the Vatican decided it would be the perfect place to set their agent.

Camper was identified early in his time at the seminary

as someone different. Someone willing to go an extra step. When he achieved the priesthood his first and last placement was at St. Pat's.

26

Camper had finally made it to the top of the stairs. It was tough, but much less pain than falling down them and he knew the sooner he stitched up his wound, the sooner he could get back to searching the files.

In the kitchen he put the kettle on. Sal always kept hordes of tea in the cupboard. He grabbed a mug and sat down to catch his breath. It was getting on two o'clock in the morning. He should have had the rest of the night to go through the place and if it came down to it he could sleep there as well, since the door was hidden. And if the cops found him, he supposed he could always claim sanctuary, but it wasn't the cops he was worried about. Sal had been possessed for years and who knew how it had happened? Maybe he was sitting in the kitchen, waiting for the kettle to boil when suddenly he heard a whisper; a whisper in the back of his head and a feeling like being smothered or falling asleep. And then he wasn't himself anymore. He was no longer Sal. He was a thing of pure evil dressed in a mask of good. Camper shuddered. The kettle began to whistle. He took out his gun and laid it on the table. He poured himself a cup and let it sit while looking through the drawers for a needle and thread. There had to be some there somewhere.

27

Gamby had gone out cold when she realized who the strange man was. When she finally woke she was lying on her own couch. A kettle was boiling in the kitchen and she had a damp cloth on her head. She didn't remember coming home. All she remembered was seeing Jeremy Daniels on the street. She reached for her gun. She'd been disarmed. This was bad. Very bad. She tried to stand. If she could just get to her phone.

"Do you take sugar in your tea?"

The voice came from the kitchen. It was Daniels. No doubt about it. What kind of game was he playing?

"One lump."

"One lump to match the one on your head, huh?"

He smiled at the joke as he entered, carrying two cups and a plate of crackers. He was still wearing his hospital robe. Luckily he had on a pair of jeans underneath.

"I hope you don't mind. But I thought you could use it. And I didn't want to just leave you here in the state you were in."

"How did you know where I live?"

"Your wallet. You told me you wanted to go home,

so since you were passed out I checked your wallet. Your keys were in your coat. Was that okay?"

Was that okay? It certainly was not, but she was disarmed, alone and at the mercy of a possibly deranged killer.

"Would you like some butter for your crackers?"

"Yes. Yes, thank you. It's in the fridge."

Daniels smiled reassuringly and left for the kitchen. He grabbed a cracker first and popped it into his mouth. As soon as he was in the kitchen Gamby tried to stand. It was hard work and made her dizzy, but she had to move. The fridge door opened and he poked his head inside.

"So tell me Detective, have you found Camper King yet?"

Gamby's eyes widened. Her insides felt all funny, like a really bad hangover. She fell to the couch and the pain went away. That was odd. That shouldn't have happened.

"Don't bother getting up. It'll just hurt. Really it's more for my protection than yours."

Gamby looked around for some reason, some explanation for her inability to move. A bottle of poison maybe. Or a syringe. Her eyes ran across the table and caught a glimpse of something marked on the floor. A circle, drawn out in what looked like blood. That had to be it. This guy was the killer. He had to be.

"It's ketchup actually. But it still does the trick."

Daniels had returned from the kitchen with a tub of butter and a knife. Gamby eyed it warily. He put down the tub and started making little cracker and butter sandwiches, stacking them up on top of each other.

"I'll take a wild guess and say you haven't found him

yet."

"That would be about right."

Daniels crunched down a cracker and took a sip of tea.

"Have you ever seen those contests in bars where you have to eat a mouthful of crackers and drink a beer and then whistle a tune? Whoever does it fastest gets a prize."

"We had them in my home town."

He took another cracker.

"So here we are Vanessa. You and me, crackers and tea, the light of the moon and a rock soundtrack from across the street. Not a bad Friday night."

Gamby had had enough. If he was going to do something he had better just do it.

"Just tell me what you want."

He looked her in the eyes, just for a second mirroring the look she had gotten from the Doctor.

"I want to tell you the truth."

She sat back on the couch and held her head.

"All of it."

At this point, she was almost ready to believe him.

28

Camper found a colour to his liking and sewed up the wound in his leg. He wished there was a drop of alcohol in the place, but apparently even *possessed* Sal didn't touch the stuff. More than once he almost passed out. There was too much at stake though; his own sanity for one thing. He didn't really care about clearing his name, after all he had actually done the stuff that they said – most of it anyway- he was just interested in the things he didn't know about. All the things he was being used for. That's what gave him the chills. He had been a puppet, he knew that, but he had been a puppet controlled by a puppet. And he wanted a piece of the hand that was behind it all; even if it meant losing his mind doing it.

He got back to his feet and tried the leg. The stitches would hold. That was good. And an overturned broom would make it easier getting around, even if it was a bit prickly. As he adjusted the broom under his arm, the handle caught a table leg and sent his tea cup to the floor, breaking the silence. He looked around for a minute, expecting the place to suddenly swarm with cops, Satanists, demons and Vatican agents. No such swarming.

But something odd *did* happen. The little puddle of tea was disappearing, being sucked down a crack in the floor. A crack where there shouldn't have been one.

With a great deal of effort and pain, he bent down to examine the floor. A crack ran in a straight line about 3 feet, then moved forty five degrees for about another 3 feet. And then again, terminating where it started. He wondered why he had never noticed it before. He'd lived there himself as parish priest years ago. The cops hadn't noticed it either. It was a hatch in the perfect shape of a triangle. There was no handle, but Camper was able to pry a knife into the crack enough to get his fingers under. He couldn't believe it. Right there under his feet. He almost knew what he was going to find before he even lifted the hatch. Maybe he was just looking in the wrong place. The key to everything could be right under the linoleum. He took a deep breath and lifted.

29

The cab pulled up to the church. Colt handed the driver a twenty.

"So, are you a sight*seer*?"

The cabbie had put an emphasis on seer that made Colt uncomfortable.

"No. I'm a local."

And he was taking his dead time making change.

"Ah. See I figured since this place is closed, and that murder happened here a few nights ago that you might be one of *those* tourists."

"What tourists?"

This was taking too long. His brain was on fire. Camper King was close. Real close.

"You know. Those people who go around looking at places where murders happened. Like that house where the woman axed her whole family. Pay a couple hundred bucks and you can even sleep in her bed. Creepy if you ask me."

He was just about to leave the cab when the driver finally handed him his change.

"Take my advice, man. Leave him alone."

Before Colt could say anything, the cab drove off. Leave him alone? What was that supposed to mean? He shrugged it off and tried the front door. Locked of course. Around back he found an easier entrance. It looked like somebody was already inside. The door had been jammed with a chair, but gave way easily. Colt took out his gun and crept through the doorway. He was in a little church kitchen, probably part of the rectory. There was a broken tea cup on the floor. And an open trap door. Could be a cellar, but it was a strange place for one. Especially in the middle of the kitchen floor and with a triangle shaped door covered in the same linoleum as the rest of the place. He approached the hole and pointed his gun down. Camper was in there. He knew it. All the signs in his head pointed to yes. Leaving his Meta-state he took his knife out and held it in his other hand. He wanted to be ready for anything.

30

"Sorry. We're closed."

Phil tried calling out to the man out front, but he couldn't hear him. He took out his phone and made a call. A few minutes later he pulled away from the store in a cab. Phil sighed and looked over the damage. His insurance wasn't covering it. And he wasn't surprised. Giant devil dogs weren't exactly in his policy. He grabbed a broom and started absently sweeping the rubble from around the counter. This wasn't the first time something like this had happened. His father had owned a shop back in the fifties, called North City Convenience. It lasted all of one day. He could still see the fires in his mind if he set himself to it. Supposedly it was caused by a lightening strike, which was ridiculous. It had been a clear day. Clear as anything. Well, they rebuilt the shop and lightening struck again. The chances of that happening was on the bad half of a billion to one. His father had sold everything to try it one more time. They even changed the name of the place to 'American Style Convenience' – a little joke about the shops in his father's home country. And this one stayed up. Even survived the big tornado of '63. And that was saying something. It passed right by the shop, moseying down the street like it was Sunday afternoon window shopping. It shouldn't have happened. And no one could really explain it, but the Weather Office said that the twister had tapered off when it got to Hudson Street and when it passed it grew again, back to a killer F5. Damnedest thing, but Phil's father swore the twister actually *smiled* at him when it passed. Needless to say it wasn't a story he repeated often and Phil himself only heard it in the hospital a few days before the old man passed on. He made him swear never to change the name of the store. Said that it was good luck. Some good luck. There was a sudden knock on the door and Phil almost dropped his broom.

"Sorry we're closed!"

Couldn't anybody read? But then he recognized the face in the window. It was that cop. The young fella. What was his name? He went to the door, making his way around the rubble and trashed merchandise, and took out his keys. The cop was in plain clothes and wearing a sling.

"Sorry Officer, I didn't know it was you."

"That's okay."

"I'm afraid there's not much left to the place. I could scrounge a can of pop or a chocolate bar for you…"

"Something to drink would be fine, thanks."

Phil picked his way through the back of the store to the cooler. Most of it was intact. He grabbed a can. Rick. His name was Rick.

"So what brings you back here, Rick?"

"Well, I know Detective Gamby already questioned

you about what happened."

"That she did."

"Yeah. She questioned me too. I know there are things you didn't tell her."

Phil shifted uncomfortably. Cop or no cop, he knew where his loyalties lay.

"Look. I'm not here as a cop. I'm here as someone who wants to help. I believe Camper King is a good man. What's happened to him isn't right. I want to find him. And I need your help."

"You want to find him and arrest him."

"No. No, you've got it wrong. I want to help him clear his name."

Phil gripped his broom. Something was welling up inside him. Anger maybe. Loyalty. He felt a little like a serf protecting a king.

"Please. I know he couldn't have done those things."

The store clerk picked up a can of loose peas from the floor, laid it on the counter and went back to his sweeping.

"I'm sorry officer but we're closed."

"I'm begging you. He saved my life. Let me help him."

Phil breathed deep and stopped sweeping.

"Then leave him alone."

"Why? I have to know."

"Because he's done everything the police are blaming him for. And you should be glad he's done those things."

31

Gamby sat back. Her mind was swimming, doing the backstroke even. Jeremy had pretty much finished off the crackers during his sermon. Boy that guy could talk.

"So. Now you know. I'm an ex-Satanist – well, *recovering* Satanist maybe, King is a Vatican agent with selective memory loss, Father Detore was King's connection with his bosses, until he got himself killed and oh, I'm from the East End. Did I leave anything out?"

"So Camper is like Buffy on a permanent acid trip?"

"No. Well. Kind of? To be honest I've never seen the show."

"And he kills vampires."

"Well, yes. And a lot more besides. Demons, werewolves, imps, zombies, hobgoblins. You name it."

"I don't believe in any of that."

"Well, you'd better start. Because it's going to get a whole lot worse. That creature that attacked King in the convenience store? Not something you see everyday. Hell hounds are very rarely used to kill humans."

"Hell hounds? This is...I just..."

"Listen. Forget everything you've read about Hell in

the Bible or in Milton or seen on television. Forget about the whole war between Heaven and Hell bit, okay. That ended a long time ago. They say that War is Hell, right?"

She couldn't believe she was listening to this.

"Well Hell is War. And the worst kind of war."

"What's that?"

"A civil war. It pits comrades against each other. Fathers against sons. Brother against brother. It's the worst war. That's what Hell is all about. It's not a dictatorship, no matter what you might think. And it's certainly not a democracy."

"Okay. Well what about - I can't believe I'm asking this - Satan? Isn't he the…guy? Why else would you be, you know, worshiping him?"

"Yes. He *is* the biggest of the bad. The original nasty, but he's sort of stepped out of the war. Sitting back and enjoying the view. Reaping the benefits so to speak. Among other things."

Daniels sat back. Clearly he was leaving some things out. She made sure to make a mental note of that.

"But there are others as well. The Lord of Worms. The Hanged Man. The Thousand Needles. All vying for control."

"And how do they do that?" She hated to ask.

"Souls my dear. Souls."

The band across the street suddenly switched to Don't Fear the Reaper. Gamby almost laughed.

"I love this song."

"You would."

She grabbed the last cracker. "So Camper King has been cracking down on their supplies, is that it?"

"Kind of. See the past few years someone's been sticking their nose in. Making Camper do things he shouldn't have been doing. Helping out one side more than the other."

"But who?" She didn't even want to think about it, but she had to ask. This was her town after all.

"No way to know. Not until he shows his face."

Gamby closed her eyes and held her head. Lord of Worms? Thousand Needles? What if it didn't even have a face?

32

Camper inched his way down the stairs in the kitchen. He left the broom where it was since it would have just gotten in the way and started carefully hopping down each step. The stairs went deeper than he thought and twice he actually had to stop to catch his breath. He was pretty sure he was even below the cellar now. A million thoughts were running through his mind about what could be at the bottom and none of them were good. He thought back to Sal. How many times had the old priest walked down these stairs? Scared and unable to stop himself? Whatever he found, it was going to get an ass kicking.

Finally there was a light. Camper hopped from the last step. He was in a tomb or catacomb of some sort, but unlike anything he had ever seen in a church. It smelled like old bread. Light was coming from an arched passageway on one wall, flickering like candles. He took out his gun and tried leaning on his leg. It would do for now. No point in going back up. Whatever had happened to Sal, it had happened down here. That meant that whatever had been controlling him also came from here. And it was time for some serious Dirty Harry payback. He checked his pocket. The ritual bone was still there. That could come in handy. And his knife was tucked into his belt. Lucky it hadn't stabbed him in the fall down the stairs. He had six silver shots in his gun and a few more rounds in the leather pouch stuffed in his pocket. Should be enough. He looked up the stairs one more time and turned toward the archway.

That was when he felt a sharp pain on the back of his head. And everything went black.

33

When the city charter was signed in 1893 there were three men present: Thomas Jacob, mayor and undertaker; Father Paul Preston, parish priest; and Dickie Mills, a former farm worker. Dickie Mills was also the town drunk. People called him Dirty Dickie behind his back. He had come from a long line of town drunks and none of his forebears had lasted much longer than thirty five years of age. Dickie was a rare forty. Mayor Jacob and Father Preston arranged the place that the signing would occur. It was in an old abandoned root cellar. Dickie didn't question it. Who was he to question the mayor and the local priest? No one in his family had ever done anything worthwhile or important. And here he was being asked to witness the signing of a city charter. People would remember him.

Dickie found the cellar alright, opened the door and stepped inside. The ceiling was vaulted and tall enough that you could stand up inside.

"Hello Dirty Dickie."

It was the mayor. He was wearing something like a monk's robe. Maybe it was a traditional thing. He'd never done anything like this before. Father Preston was standing next to him. There were candles lit and a low table lay between them.

"Just Dickie yer Honour, if it's no trouble."

"Fine. Fine."

The priest looked nervous. He was fiddling with his collar as if the place was too warm, but it wasn't. In fact it was quite cold. Dickie started to think how warm it was in the pub.

"Can we just get on with it Thomas?"

"Of course Father, of course."

Dickie moved toward the table. There was a piece of paper laid out, folded over book like. And a pen.

"What do I have to do yer Honour?"

"Just stand right there Dirty Dickie."

"I'm sorry yer Honour, please don't call me –"

Dickie Mills fell to the floor of the root cellar, a long white knife sticking out of his back. No one would ever remember him or his family. Father Preston retrieved his blade. He took out a piece of cloth and wiped the blade clean.

"Now Father. Let's get on with this. Would you mind dipping the pen in Dickie's wound? I have a dinner to attend in an hour and I've got to get home and get changed."

34

Camper woke in a sweat. He was still below the church, but his hands were bound. He had been disarmed and his head was aching. There was still a light coming from the archway, but he couldn't hear anyone inside. Who had attacked him? No one could have known he was here. Then he heard the creak of the trapdoor opening and footsteps descending. He quickly closed his eyes, feigning unconsciousness and listened as carefully as he could.

"I found him down here."

"Well let's have a look at him."

There were two voices. Both male. One older than the other and perhaps the first's ordinate. The footsteps grew louder and Camper swallowed the temptation to peek. He needed information and it was better if they thought he was still out cold. One thing was for certain: these were neither cops nor demons. He had no idea who they were.

"I didn't really expect him to be bald, but then I didn't really know what to expect."

"I found these on him."

"You were lucky."

"Well, he was already injured."

Yeah and I had my back turned.

"What's down that tunnel?"

"I haven't checked it yet. Probably more of the same."

"Go have a look, Colt. Might be important."

Camper could hear footsteps going down the tunnel, then another set stepping toward him. Here it comes.

"You can open your eyes now Camper, if you wish. No use pretending."

How did he know? Camper opened his eyes. A large man in a dark coat was standing above him. He had glasses pushed down to the tip of his nose.

"I know because I know lots of things."

A telepath. Had to be. Camper tried emptying his mind of everything.

"It's not much good doing that. Doesn't really affect what I can do. Now if you don't mind, I'm going to have a bit of a closer look inside your brain before handing you over to the police."

The man got closer to Camper and laid his hands on his head. At once Camper felt a terrible headache, like someone was forcing his skull open with a pair of rusty pliers.

"Someone's been in here before."

The man's face grew dark and more focused.

"They've been here very often. And didn't want anyone else to know. Including you. But the walls are weakening."

His eyes suddenly went wide.

"Did you know about this?!"

Camper screwed up his face. Of course he knew. Telepath or no this guy was kind of slow.

"You've been a very bad boy Camper. Gamby is right. You're the one. And you belong behind bars."

The man removed his hands and backed away. Camper's headache had almost disappeared. He blinked a few times to try to clear his head and as he blinked a shadow crept from the tunnel. The light went out and there was the sound of a dull, wet thud and then something hitting the floor.

"Well Camper. Looks like it's just you and me now."

It was the voice of the other man. Colt. Only changed. Darker and deeper. Familiar somehow.

"You got the drop on me once, but it looks like this time you're all tied up."

A hand grabbed him and started dragging him across the floor.

"Come on. My Master is waiting."

35

Eddie Tripper didn't mean to eavesdrop, it just happened by accident. Ask anybody. He was just doing his duties, sweeping up the hall in The Circle. A door was opened and he just kept sweeping through. It wasn't until he looked up that he realized he shouldn't have been there - that he was standing smack dab in the middle of the Library of the Three. Well, the Library of the Two for now. And when he heard voices he did what anyone would have done. He looked for a place to hide.

"This could ruin us all, Voracious."

The slim and sharp Voracious wasn't even bothering to look at Malicious, who was pacing like a man possessed. He knew what had to be done, but he wanted to see if the other man could figure it out on his own. And anyway, it would be better if it were someone else's idea.

"If Salacious goes public about the group, we're finished! A hundred and fifty years of secrecy down the drain. If my father were here-"

"But your father isn't. The old ones give themselves to the Great One. And we continue to serve. That's the way it's done."

"So what are we supposed to do about it?"

"I don't know."

"You've got the center chair *Alfred*, it's your decision."

Voracious had no idea how Malicious had gotten hold of his real name, but even that wasn't going to budge him. And having the center chair was just the beginning. If he played this right, there wouldn't be any other chairs. The way it should have been all along.

"Whatever we decide to do, we have to do it fast."

Malicious kicked the floor. No way were they even thinking about it, but then again, he was sure The Circle had done worse during his father's time. Okay. If that was the way it had to be, then so be it.

"Salacious has to die."

"Are you sure, Malicious?"

"It's the only way. We can't let him talk."

Voracious smiled inwardly.

"What do you have in mind?"

Eddie listened as closely as he dared and when the pair finally left he crept from his closet hiding space and exited the library. He was full of questions and there was no one he could go to for answers. Well. There was one person. Not someone he wanted to see, and not someone who wanted to see him, but that was that. He didn't have any other choice. Maybe the old man would know what to do.

36

"I'm definitely buying Ventnor Avenue."

Jeremy groaned. "But I need it for the set!"

"Well, we'll just have to deal. But not until I pass GO again."

He picked up the dice. It had been a long night and neither one of them felt like sleeping. He had removed the circle from the floor and had struck a truce with the detective. They would work together to find Camper and get to the bottom of the killings. She still wasn't sure if she believed everything he had said, but she had seen enough to suspect that some of it might be true. She had even given him a tee shirt to wear so he could ditch the hospital gown. It had a unicorn on it.

"Doubles again, looks like you're going to jail, Salacious."

"Jeremy. Please."

Gamby laughed for the first time in days. Then a knock came to the door. They both looked at each other. She checked her watch. It was three o'clock in the morning. Who the hell could that be?

She reached for her gun – Jeremy had hidden it in the

fridge – and looked out through the peephole.

"I can't believe it. What are you doing here?"

She opened the door and Rick walked in, with Phil the convenience store clerk in tow. They both took a double take at Jeremy, sitting on the floor in front of a Monopoly board, with a plate of buttered crackers next to him.

"It's okay Rick. He's alright. I think. He's gonna help me find Camper."

She had decided early on not to tell anyone about the Society. The more people she had looking, the better, but she didn't want them more involved than they had to be.

"That's why I'm here. I've got some info, but you probably won't believe a word of it."

Phil stepped forward. He had made a promise years ago. A promise to the man who had saved his life. Twice. And now he was breaking it to save his. There was no other way. Gamby motioned them to sit down.

"Wanna bet?"

37

"So what's the story? Are you going to torture me? Or kill me straight? For some reason I get the feeling you're more into the torture, but I'd like to put my vote in for killing me straight away. I get really annoying when I'm being tortured. I talk a lot. Make jokes. A lot of sarcasm. You wouldn't want to hear that."

Camper was being dragged by his ankles down a tunnel. There was candlelight ahead of him. The man called Colt looked back and smiled. There was something about him. Something about him that seemed so... Sal. Now he knew. The demon that had been in Sal. This guy may have come into St. Pat's in his right mind, but he wasn't in control anymore. Whatever had been inside Sal for all those years was now inside Colt. And was dragging Camper to God knew where.

"I can tell by your expression that you've figured it out. That's good Camper. Good. I was kind of hoping it would have been you to find the altar. Then I could have taken you. That would have been fun. But this body is fine too. It has talents. Talents I might have a use for in time."

Camper gritted his teeth as he was dragged across the

stone and gravel of the tunnel. He was almost sure his wound was bleeding now. He could feel a warm sensation running down his leg.

"The time that I wasted on you. Do you know what it was like? Confined in that old man all those years? Doing his daily tasks so as not to arouse suspicion? I had to perform Mass! Not to mention the occasional baptism and wedding. Not very often. But often enough. Can you imagine what that must have been like? A demon of hell, trapped in the body of an old priest, being forced to hand out communion to old ladies? Shake hands with new parents and comfort the bereaved? I felt like tearing my eyes out! I nearly did a few times..."

"Sorry."

"You'll be sorry. My Master wants you back in the fold, but we have to start from scratch to do that. And before we wipe you clean, I'm gonna have some fun. You might not like it Camper, but I promise you won't remember a thing. In fact, the only thing you'll be wondering is where you got the new scars."

Things were just getting better and better. He had to keep the demon talking if he was going to get out of there. Demons loved to talk. That was something he knew. Especially when things were going their way. And Camper needed information. He was bound to slip.

38

Phil sat on the couch. He looked at the floor.

"Who's winning?"

"Jeremy, but I think he's cheating."

The detective smiled and Phil found himself relaxing a little. This was tough, but he was sure he'd be forgiven for it. He had to be. He was a good man after all.

"Just tell her everything you told me."

Rick kept on eye trained on Salacious. He couldn't believe Gamby was trusting him. They must have made some kind of deal.

"Well. It has to do with the City charter."

Jeremy perked up. There were things he hadn't told Gamby. Secrets he wasn't ready to reveal yet. It looked like there was more to Phil than met the eye.

"What about the Charter?" Gamby was getting inpatient.

"I'm talking about the *real* Charter. Not the one at City Hall. The *other* one."

"What are you talking about?"

"My father's first store, it was built back in the fifties. There was a land dispute you see. Our family owned the land. My father bought it fair and square, but someone showed up with papers saying that it belonged to the city. So my father went to city hall to look into it. He was a smart man, my father. PhD. He found out the city didn't have any rights to the land. Some kind of cover up, but that wasn't all he found out. He was curious to a fault, always had been. Old city maps were full of discrepancies that weren't adding up, so he started digging. Eventually figured out that the city charter itself was a fraud. No one believed him. Who would? It was hard on him, but he managed to pay the right people so he could keep the land and build the store. He didn't have much luck. He didn't have much luck with that one. Or the second store. Sold everything he had to start the third. Even the house. We lived above the store for years. Hell, I still do."

Salacious clutched his paper money tightly. Come on man. If you're going to spill it, then spill it.

"A few years ago I went looking into it. Dad had told me the story and I started to do some snooping around. It wasn't fair, you know? I thought if I could get some proof... I mean, Dad had been gone for a while but I felt I owed it to him to try. Probably shouldn't have. It got me into more trouble than I'd ever been in. If it hadn't been for Camper King – Do you think I could have a glass of water?"

Gamby got up and headed for the kitchen. Rick, his eyes still on Salacious, helped himself to a cracker. Rookie or no, he could tell that Phil's story was starting to bother him. If anything was going to happen, he'd be ready for it.

Gamby came back from the kitchen with a mug shaped like a pig. *Shepherd's Grove High '72* was emblazoned on the side. Jeremy grinned.

"Nice."

She kicked over his only hotel.

"It was a gift."

Phil took a sip and cleared his throat.

"Camper King saved me. If it wasn't for him I wouldn't be here."

"What did he do?"

"I tracked down the Charter, the right one. Figured I'd finally make the thing public, but I couldn't get to it. It was being held, protected by some group called The Circle."

Salacious winced. Here it comes.

"I tried to get it. Even found out where they were keeping it, but they had people there. And they took me. Had me laid out on a table like something out of Temple of Doom. Dagger raised and everything. Then Camper showed up. Out of nowhere. Him and his silver gun. I know, I know. It sounds pretty crazy saying it out loud like this. But it happened. It happened just like I said."

Phil took another sip of his water. "I kinda wish this was a beer right now."

"What happened then?

Gamby knew there had to be more.

"He brought me home. Told me about himself. A little about what he did. Not everything though. You could ask him about it and what he did after that, but you'll only get a dumb look. He forgot about the whole thing. Next time I saw him come into the store he didn't even know who I was. So I always did my best to be friendly to him."

"And what about the Charter?"

"I don't know, but from what he told me Camper only

forgets the things he's done when they happen to be really nasty. The kind of thing that will stay with you. Affect you for the rest of your life. Whatever he did after he left me at home that night must have been terrible. That's the only explanation for him not being able to remember it."

Gamby looked down at the floor. Jeremy was putting down his paper money. They were soaking with sweat.

"Well, Jeremy. Perhaps it's time you told us what The Circle is really all about."

39

The little apartment was barely big enough for one person, but Eddie's father had called it home for the last ten years, ever since he had quit The Circle. Suddenly his work contacts were failing him. Every deal was collapsing. Every *t* was failing to get crossed and every *i* was missing a dot. And his receding hairline was receding even further to top it all off. So he gave up. Left his family – they were being ruined anyway – and faked his own death. It was the only thing that actually worked for him. He suspected his former friends might have had something to do with it. Better that he appeared dead.

Eddie knocked on the door. He had tracked down his father three years ago, shortly after joining The Circle. He had heard a rumour in the group about a former member who had faked his own death and Eddie had always had his suspicions. He was a smart kid. When he found his father he was thrown out the door. The second time he visited, to tell him about his Mom's death, his father made him a coffee. He stayed a half an hour and they spoke very little. The last thing his father said to him was *don't come back*. Well. There goes that.

"Who is it?"

"It's Eddie."

Silence. Eddie started to wonder if it was a bad idea coming here.

"Who's dead now?"

"No one, Dad. Let me in."

There was the sound of footsteps toward the door.

"Why should I?"

"I have some questions. Come on Dad, open up."

The door opened slightly. The security chain was still attached. A wrinkled face appeared in the crack in the door.

"What kind of questions?"

"Circle questions."

Eddie's father slammed the door hard, leaving Eddie in the hall. He knew he should have waited. He should have waited until he was inside, *then* ask him. Damn it.

Just as Eddie was turning to leave, the door slowly opened. His father appeared.

"Don't call me Dad. I told you. Call me Chuck if you're going to call me anything. The neighbours could be listening."

He beckoned the young man inside. Not so young anymore he had to remind himself. And a member of The Circle too. That was important.

"So what's this about?"

"I...overheard something. Something I shouldn't have. Dad – Chuck...they're going to kill someone."

Eddie's Dad looked his son deep in the eyes. Then he raised his hand and punched him in the shoulder.

"How long have you been with The Circle, boy? Don't

you know by now that's what they do? They sacrifice. *Sacrifice*. It's one of their primary functions. Or at least it used to be. Haven't you seen it happen?"

"No. Not yet, I guess. I just entered the Seventh Circle. Up until now I haven't seen anything really."

"Three years and you've only now entered the Seventh. It's a good thing that I'm dead."

"Well, what Circle were you then?"

"Doesn't matter."

"Fine."

"Alright. If you must know, Third."

Eddie was shocked. He had no idea that is father had been a member of the Third Circle.

"I saw things that I will never forget. If you're smart you'll get out now. You'll get out now before it ruins you like it ruined me."

"Dad – "

"Chuck."

"Chuck, the man they're going to kill, he used to sit in the center chair."

The old man's eyes widened. That was strange. Never heard something like that happening before. What was going on down there anyway? The functions of The Circle were pretty clear cut. Nothing like this should have ever happened.

"They're afraid he'll reveal something about the group to the public. I don't know what it is, but I heard them mention a charter. Isn't that like a set of laws?"

If Chuck was surprised before, then he was going into shock now. He looked around him, as if something might creep up from behind and then ran to the curtains, closing them quickly.

"Are you sure no one knows that you're here?"

Eddie nodded.

"Are you absolutely sure?"

"I'm sure."

"Because if you're not more sure of this than anything you've ever been in your life then we're both dead men."

Chuck sat on the couch. His hands were shaking. Eddie got him a glass of water.

"You don't know *evil,* boy. Until now you've been playing games. Make-believe. You haven't seen it. And please God you won't."

"What is it Dad? What is the Charter?"

Chuck took a deep breath. He knew just by talking about it he was putting his son in danger, but there was nothing that could be done. Sooner or later he'd dig up the information and say the wrong thing to the wrong person and then that would be it. He already knew too much. No. This was the safest thing to do.

"It's a contract, Eddie. A contract between the city and Hell itself."

Eddie gulped.

40

Camper dug his heels into the floor as hard as he could to slow Colt down. It worked a little, but he received a boot in the ribs for his efforts. That was okay. Delay him all you can. Stall. Stall for what? No one knew he was there. He wanted it that way so he could hide out. Well, perhaps the Deus ex Machina would show up in the nick of time. Yeah. With donuts and a double double.

"You've gotten quiet old man. Feeling guilty? You know I could hear your confession for you if you like."

Colt swung around, dropping Camper to the stone floor.

"You want me to confess? Camper the things I've done in ten lifetimes would make you scream for death. You'd beg me to take your life now so you wouldn't have to think about what I've done. That's how horrible I am."

He smiled.

"Now the things *you've* done for me have been pretty awful as well. I was curious if any of those memories had gotten back in. Since you killed the priest and I had to wait for another host I thought you might get some back."

Camper's mind filled with images of the little girl.

Broken and bleeding. The smell of his gunshot in the air.

"No. I'm a blank slate."

"Too bad. That would have made things even more fun."

Camper tried to think of a way to keep Colt talking, but his mind was fixed on the little girl. How many others had he killed to appease some demon or devil? How many lives had he taken that deserved to live?

"Here we are!"

Camper raised his head. Just as he thought. There was a demonic altar buried beneath the Church. Sal must have stumbled on it years ago and been possessed by that thing. That foul thing. Then when Colt went to investigate the tunnel the same thing happened to him. It really was lucky that Camper hadn't gone in first.

The room had a vaulted ceiling. It was low, but with enough room to stand up. There was an altar against one wall with candles and a silver plate resting in the center. The walls themselves were carved with every manner of horrific symbolism. Camper recognized a few images. This was an altar to the Hanged Man. A demon of Hell. And not one of the nice ones.

"Like it Camper? You've been here before, but you don't remember it. Did you know that the city Charter was signed in this very room? It was nothing but a root cellar then. Makes me feel all tingly inside just thinking about it."

"The city Charter?"

"You know about the Charter. Don't you remember? You tried to steal it from The Circle years ago. Idiots. Didn't go so well from what I recall."

That was it. Exactly what he needed. Now he just had to keep him going. If he was going to die here at least he'd get to find out why.

"I have no idea what you're talking about."

"Okay Camper. I'll give in. We both know you'll forget everything I say anyway, so it doesn't really matter, but let's call it a favour. For all the good work you've done for us."

Colt sat on the floor next to him with his legs crossed, like someone about to tell a campfire story.

"The Charter is what makes this city so great. The Charter is what gives my Master the right to do business here."

"Business?"

"Lucifer has the right to tempt every creature on this planet for its soul. And he can also accept sacrifices. And it's those souls that give him his power, that make him great. But things started changing in Hell not long ago. Other Demons started to gain strength. A civil war erupted. The Devil liked it. War is his domain after all and he knew that he was untouchable. But he didn't want one side to become more powerful than the others. So he struck a bargain with them. Another one of his fortés."

"What kind of bargain?"

"He would give them access to the souls on earth in order to fuel their war. The conditions were such that he remains ruler if the war ever ends and that the souls may only be tempted or sacrificed from a place of his choosing. A city with no name."

"The Dot."

"Exactly. Your city's founding fathers signed a contract

in blood in this very room and ever since then the greater demons of hell have been tempting and killing and doing whatever else they like. My Master is a bit of a party crasher himself."

"So what did the founding fathers get out of it?"

"Oh the usual. Fame. Riches. Women. They lived their mortal lives in glory and wealth and then they died and their souls were eaten by the Great One. Such is the way of the world."

"So that's why I was hired. That's why this city is rotting on the inside."

"That's a nice way of putting it. Yes. You'd been hunting and investigating for five years, causing us a whole lot of trouble and then along came Sal. He was exactly what we were looking for."

Ten years. They had Sal in their grip for ten years. He would never forgive them for it.

"You were at the edge. Almost delusional, but not quite. There were some who wanted to leave you be. Let the madness take you. Then we could get back to business. My Master had other plans. The Vatican were worried about you. They didn't want to lose such a strong fighter. Enter, Father Sal Detore. Are you writing all this down?"

If only he had his hands free. He'd wipe that smile off of Colt's face with a knife.

"Detore had been working as a missionary and got in real deep with Voodoo. He had a price on his head, did you know? His talents were just what the Vatican ordered. You were retired from your duties at St. Pat's and the old priest stepped in. You'd do a job, write a report and then Detore would file the report and wipe the memory away.

My Master had an altar here, a place where I could pass through. You had been too far gone to influence, but Detore, let's just leave his past in the past. It only took a few whispers. A scattered word. It was almost too perfect when the priest walked into this room and I took over. For all his faith there was nothing he could do. And everything you've done since then has been for my Master. It's all been to make the Hanged Man number two in Hell."

Colt took a deep breath and stretched, like a professor after a long lecture.

"And now, dear Camper, we're going to get you back. I learned enough while I was inside Detore to wipe your memory clean. We're going to start from scratch. Right here and now."

Colt turned and faced the altar. He started to mutter some words in a language Camper didn't recognize, raising his arms in the air. He didn't hear the man running down the tunnel, or entering the room. Camper himself hardly heard him, he was so intent on what Colt was doing, looking for an opening – any opening. Before he knew what was happening Colt felt a sharp pain in his lower back that spread upwards. He fell over instantly, cursing Camper King with every last breath. Camper looked up at the man who had just saved his life and probably hundreds more. Things were getting shadowy. Light was moving in and out. There wasn't much time. He had to get to his feet.

"Untie me! Now!"

A set of hands appeared behind him and untied his bonds. Camper got to his feet. The next few minutes went by quickly and in a haze. He was working completely on instinct and fumes. His lips moving frantically in prayer. When the ritual was completed and his energies finally spent he fell to the floor. Everything went dark. If this was the end he didn't mind. He knew what had happened. He finally had the answer. Perhaps he deserved to die for everything that he had done. If he had been stronger he would have known. Could have stopped it maybe. No. This was right. The demon was gone. Sal had been avenged and now the little girl would be avenged. The little girl whose name he didn't even know. It was the right time to die.

Or it would have been.

41

Jeremy sat back. Now they knew everything he did; everything about The Circle and its illustrious history. The Circle was created for the sole purpose of protecting the Charter. That was it. Everything else was extraneous. A hundred odd years of keeping that document secret. Camper King tried to get it, years ago, and failed. And for some reason he had never tried again. Jeremy had never understood why.

They sat there in silence for a moment, as if entranced by the Monopoly game. Rick was the first to speak.

"So what happens if someone gets the Charter?"

"Nothing really. Unless they destroy it."

Gamby picked up the dice and threw them down.

"And what then?"

"Certain doors are closed. The deal is forfeit. And whoever is to blame will end up with a big target on their back."

"A big target?"

"Well, think about it. This deal gives the greater demons of Hell rights to traffic souls in the city. With the Charter gone, they're back to nothing, but that doesn't mean that they're shut out completely. They'll send their emissaries to exact revenge on whoever destroys the Charter."

Gamby stifled a laugh and shook her head. She was still having trouble swallowing all of this.

"This is serious. I've been with The Circle long enough to have seen some crazy things happen. And you all saw the hell hound in his convenience store. This is old time stuff. It's dark and deep and above all, it's real."

Applause erupted from the bar across the street as the local band finished their last set. Phil could see the lights being turned on through the window, a polite way of telling the patrons to go home.

"What exactly did you do for The Circle anyway?"

Salacious spoke slowly and in a whisper, almost to himself.

"I was their leader."

42

Eddie left the old man's place looking over his shoulder. It was late, but Chuck hadn't offered the couch. Figured. Tell your son all about the evils of the city and then send him home at three thirty in the morning to walk alone in the dark. Eddie wasn't a coward, not by any means, but he was slim. Not slim and trim. Not Bruce Lee slim. He was just a little guy. A little guy walking in a not-so-nice part of town in the middle of the night. Proof positive that even Satanists can be afraid of the dark, given the right circumstances.

So the city made a deal with the Devil. He supposed stranger things had happened. One of the initiates had told him about a man in Texas who wanted his dog to join the Devil's pack. The dog was going to die and this guy called up Satan to take him. To take the dog and let him join the Great Hunt. According to the story, the dog was taken alright. Became a hound of hell. And then came back and ate his former owner. Seems the man used to beat him daily and sending the poor thing to hell was just the final straw in a lifetime of abuse. The initiate who told him the story was also fond of drawing crucifixes on other members' robes. Well, anything was possible.

Two blocks down the road Eddie made a right turn onto Lucky Lane. He should have turned left so he could catch the number six bus home, but something made him turn right. A little whisper deep in his brain. A tiny voice that he had never heard before was urging him in this direction. There was something down here he was supposed to find. He kept walking, not even really paying attention to where he was going. The whisper was so sure, so confident. He had to go this way. Keep going. Keep going. There. Stop. Now turn right. Look up. Eddie looked up. He was standing in front of a hardware store. In the window was an axe. He looked around, found a piece of loose concrete on the sidewalk and heaved it toward the window. Alarms started ringing, but Eddie couldn't hear them. Just the voice. So calm. So sure.

Take it.

He stepped up through the broken glass of the window and grabbed the axe. What was he doing? Smashing in windows and stealing things? But the voice was so reassuring. No. Just the axe. But what was he going to do with it? He listened to the whisper in his head. It told him everything he needed to know. He jumped down from the window, still holding the axe, feeling the weight of it in his hand, and ducked into an alley. The police would be there soon and he had places to be. So much to do. So very much to do.

43

When Camper finally woke he felt like he had been drinking all night. His head was pounding, but he was alive and he didn't expect that, so that was a good thing. He tried clearing his eyes and found he was in what looked like a run down motel room. He was lying on a cheap green sofa and there was a proper bandage wrapped around his leg. He looked around for his savior and then heard whistling from another room. It sounded like the Ode to Joy.

"You're awake. That's good. I made coffee."

The man that came in was dressed in jeans and a tee-shirt with a little salt and pepper cap on his head. He seemed vaguely familiar, like maybe a cab driver he had had once.

"Do you take sugar?"

Camper started to get up.

"Sugar. Do you take sugar?"

"Yeah, four lumps."

"Four lumps."

The man disappeared back into the other room. Camper checked the bandage on his leg. The Deus ex

Machina knew what he was doing. The bleeding had stopped and he probably wouldn't need a hospital after all. A second later he returned with two cups of coffee and handed one to Camper.

"So who should start first?"

Camper shrugged. His brain was still kind of fried.

"I can guess what you'd ask anyways. Who am I? What was I doing in the Church? Where are we and how did we get here? I assume a *thank you* would be in there somewhere as well."

Camper forced a smile.

"That's about it."

"Well this is my place. It's a wreck but what can you do. We got here in my cab. I'm a cab driver, my name is Michael and St. Pat's is my parish. How does that sound?"

"St. Pat's has been closed since the murder and I was in a secret basement."

"Right. Look, I thought I'd spare you the details since you're still recovering."

"No need."

"Right. Well. I suppose you should know. There's no harm in it."

"Just get on with it."

"Right. Well. I used to be part of a group. The Society for the Recognition of Meta-States."

"I've heard of it."

"You have? You shouldn't have. I mean, despite the group's name, they're actually pretty secretive."

"It's part of my business to know what's happening in The Dot."

"Of course it is. Of course. As for myself, I know all about you."

Camper raised an eyebrow.

"Well. Ahh. The group, in recent years, has been involved in some illegal activities. Small time stuff. Mostly. The head of the group has – well, had, since Colt killed him – had a penchant for the macabre. One of the reasons the group was hunting you down I imagine. He wanted a look inside your brain. He was fascinated with killers. Not that you're a killer – "

"I am a killer. Go on."

Michael took a half second to wipe the look of disbelief off of his face and then continued.

"Well. I quit the group months ago. I didn't like the way things were going. Dr. Martin had a way with convincing people in the group to do things, even if they didn't want to. I had a chance to leave, to disappear, and I took it. There was someone good at hiding, someone not part of the group. She found me and gave me the chance. Cost a lot, but it was worth it. Believe me."

Camper looked around the place in surprise.

"The state of my apartment has nothing to do with my bank account. At least it didn't until I paid up. You see she was so good at hiding that I don't even remember who she was. And the group doesn't remember who I am. "

"But this Martin guy can look inside peoples head's right?"

"She had a way around it. Something to do with her gift. I don't pretend to understand it. Not even Colt could find someone she was helping. And he was the dangerous one. He was doing things for Martin of his own accord.

He *believed* in the group. Didn't need to be coerced."

"So how did you end up in the church basement?"

"I drove Colt to St. Pat's. In my cab. It was pure luck that I picked him up. I could see the look on his face that he was after somebody. He used to get this look when he was in his Meta-State, like he was constipated. I knew whoever he was looking for was in the church and it wasn't going to be good."

"You took your dead time getting back. Not that I don't appreciate it."

"Listen, you've got to understand. My Meta-State takes me a good hour of preparation. Then I have to sit down and eat like a sumo wrestler in training. It's not pretty. And I don't like doing it. So you should be thankful I got there when I did."

He was. And he had more questions, but he was getting tired again. He had to lie down.

"Go ahead and lie down. I can see it in your face. Sleep as long as you want. I've got to hit the streets anyway."

Camper lay back on the couch. This place was as good as the Church he supposed. Michael wasn't going to call the cops and no one could connect the two of them.

"Michael?"

"Yeah?"

"What exactly can you do?"

"Well, you've heard of the Flash right?"

Camper nodded.

"Brother, he ain't got nothin' on me."

44

When Gamby got to the scene it was already crawling with forensics. She had Rick in tow. Seems he was becoming her unofficial partner. Well, as long as the Captain didn't know. To be honest she was glad he was hanging around; another normal person who had been exposed to all the craziness that they had heard last night. Jeremy was still at her place, wearing her pajamas and eating her cereal. If the Captain knew she was harboring a man wanted for questioning, letting Rick come with her to a crime scene would be the least of her worries.

"Could I have a minute here, guys?"

The lab boys gave Rick an odd look and left the room. They were standing in a little apartment; a student place if the décor was any indication – makeshift end tables, a guitar and a *periodic table of beer* poster on the wall. There were three bodies and their various pieces on the floor. It was sloppy work. Blood splatters on the walls. How did she get used to seeing this kind of thing? She wasn't sure. Her mind took over and broke down the scene in her head. Injuries probably done with an axe or machete or some other large, heavy bladed instrument. There were symbols drawn on the floor in chalk. Similar to the symbols she had seen at the other crime scenes, but different. Less precise.

Rick had wandered into one of the bedrooms. Maybe she was making a mistake letting him tag along, but it certainly couldn't hurt. For all she knew they *all* had demonic prices on their heads. Better to stick together.

"Hey Vanessa, you better take a look at this."

Gamby walked into the bedroom.

"Listen Rick, it's Gamby at work. And make it Detective if there's anyone around, okay?"

Rick nodded. He had the closet door open. Inside was not what she expected. Things just kept getting more and more complicated. Maybe she should have brought Jeremy along after all, as a consulting Satanist.

"So what do you think it means?"

Rick was holding up one of the robes from the closet, emblazoned with a circle design on the left breast. He should have been wearing gloves.

"I don't know Rick. I really don't know."

"Umm. I should probably be wearing gloves, right?"

Gamby nodded.

As Rick was putting the robe back into the closet, a small medallion fell out of it and onto the floor. Gamby bent down, taking a handkerchief out of her pocket - always carried one - and picked it up gently. She wrapped it in the cloth and put it in her pocket.

"Shouldn't that go to the lab?"

Gamby stood up.

"I think Jeremy will be able to tell us more about this than the lab. Let's let them back in to finish."

45

Camper woke up and for a second forgot that he wasn't home. He looked around. Michael hadn't come back yet. Then again, he was a taxi driver, so he could be gone the rest of the day and maybe the night too. He seemed like a nice enough fella, for a freak. Camper chuckled to himself. Look who was talking. His stomach growled and he realized he hadn't eaten since yesterday. He had to stop doing that.

The kitchen was tiny with just the bare essentials, making room for the massive refrigerator and deep freeze. Inside both was enough food to feed the National Guard. Camper couldn't believe it. Everything under the sun and in bulk too. He almost felt guilty just getting a bowl of cereal, afraid of messing the place up. No wonder the rest of the apartment was a bit run down. Michael the taxi-driver was spending it all on food. Come to think of it, it actually made sense. Trance or no trance he probably burned up a lot of carbohydrates doing everything at triple or quadruple speed. Without the energy already stored up inside him to burn off he would probably just collapse. That wasn't a pretty image, running yourself to death.

Camper found a spot next to the window, sitting at a little table and eating his cereal. It was a dingy day outside. A little bit of rain and a few clouds but still warm. The kind of day he liked. Suddenly he wondered what would happen if he turned himself in. He wanted the police to trust him, but how could he go to them when he was actually guilty? Who would believe his story? It was like something out of a movie. He didn't even believe it himself half the time. Wondering when someone would jump out from behind a fence and yell "Gotcha! April Fool's on your whole life!" But that wasn't about to happen. And where was he supposed to go from here? Where could he turn? Sal was dead. The demon was banished, possibly forever - he hoped- and the head of that *society* was gone too. He still had a price on his head. Presumably the Hanged Man wouldn't give up that easy, but what about the Vatican? Sal had been his only contact with them since the whole thing started. Wouldn't they be wondering what was going on? That was a scary thought. The last thing he needed was a swarm of Vatican agents, maybe just like him, descending on The Dot to look for him. They might blame him for all the killings, a willing disciple of the Hanged Man. It was all too much.

Camper knocked over his cereal when the door opened.

"Who wants some pizza?"

"Michael, was that really necessary?"

Michael laid three large pizzas on the table in front of Camper and noticed the cereal on the floor.

"You're tense."

"Of course I'm tense."

He bent down, grabbing a napkin from the top of one of the pizza boxes and started wiping up the milk.

"I'm the walking dead, Michael. The only way any of this is going to end is when I'm in the ground."

"Oh, I wouldn't say that. You never know what might happen next."

Michael took a big bite of pizza and smiled.

"You know something? What's going on?"

"First, you have to agree to take me with you."

Camper gave him a look that said *try again*.

"Okay. Okay. Well, at least buy me some, I don't know, some spare ribs."

"Spare ribs?"

"I'm out."

"Alright, spare ribs. What is it?"

Michael laid down his slice.

"I was talking to Vanessa Gamby today."

Camper dropped his napkin.

"What did you do?"

46

Eddie woke up in a sweat. He had no idea how he had gotten home from his father's place the previous night, but there he was, lying on his rusty old couch, still in his clothes. He cleared his throat and went to the bathroom. His reflection told him more. His eyes were dark and drawn, like he hadn't slept all night. His hair was in shambles. And running up and down the front of his shirt were dark red streaks and blobs or splatters. It looked like blood. Couldn't be, but that was what it looked like. And it didn't smell like jam.

Eddie rushed out of the bathroom, frantic and looking around his apartment for any other sign showing what he had been doing last night. His jacket was the same story, dried up red blotches on the sleeves and chest. And resting against the wall near his shoes was the proverbial smoking gun: An axe, still bloody, lay propped against the wall. He almost fainted.

The first thing he did was call his father. It took four tries before Chuck actually answered the phone. Damn call display.

"What's wrong? Why are you calling me?"

"Something happened."

"What? No, never mind. I don't want to know. Better if I don't know about any of it."

"It's real bad."

"Like I said, better if I don't know."

Eddie could almost hear his father thinking on the other end of the line. If Chuck didn't have any advice he was sunk. There was nowhere he could turn.

"Do you have any friends at The Circle?"

"Not really. One or two, but not really. Besides, this isn't something I could go to them with."

"Listen to me. It doesn't matter. That's still your best bet. Whatever's happened probably has to do with what you found out. Can't be a coincidence. You need a confidant. Someone at The Circle who can help get you out of there."

Chuck hung-up suddenly. Probably had been timing the phone call in case it was being traced or something. Crazy as he was, his advice was good. He had to get out. It was the only way, but first things first. He had to get rid of his bloody clothes, and then bury the axe that was in his porch. He wished he could remember what had happened. Was he drugged? Or maybe framed by The Circle? His thoughts rushed to the conversation he had overheard. They wanted Salacious Cain dead. Oh no.

47

"No way. It's not happening."

Camper was pacing like a man possessed. He couldn't believe his ears. Michael was persistent.

"According to my sources, she was working with the Society to track you down. If she was working with them and open to the possibility of meta-states, then she must be open to at least the *possibility* of the supernatural. She could be sympathetic to what's been happening to you."

"Or she could just throw me in jail. I don't even know what's been happening to me, how is she supposed to help?"

Michael picked up the last remnants of pizza crust and chomped on it.

"You don't get it do you? She's been investigating the *Pentagram Murders* for ten years. She might have some information you've missed."

Maybe it was true. He had gone over most of the case files, but they only gave one side of the story. The demon inside Sal had been lying to him for years about what he had been doing; sending him off to do the Hanged Man's dirty work, all under the guise of ridding the city of evil.

Jail or no jail, maybe she was the only way to get some real answers. That was something he could live with.

"When?"

"You'll actually meet her? Okay. Well, she gave me a number to call whenever you're ready. Said that it wouldn't be at the station, but at a bar."

"A bar? Now's not the time to be tricking me into a blind date, Michael. A bar. I can't believe I'm doing this."

Michael smiled.

"Just call the number. Before I change my mind."

48

"I don't think you should be alone, that's all."

Rick had been on edge ever since the phone call came in, but Gamby wasn't budging. She didn't want Camper to flinch, not for a second. The easiest way to do it was alone, in a dark and crowded place where he didn't have to worry about being identified.

"Look Rick, you'll be just across the street with Jeremy at my place. If anything happens I'll call you. We're just going to talk."

"Yeah, okay, just talk with a man accused of being the serial killer you've been investigating. Everything Jeremy and Phil told us could be a lie. Who knows? And what about those cultists who were murdered? Jeremy told us they were high ranking members according to the medallion we found. And we know that Camper has it out for that group."

"Your concern is sweet, but I'm still the detective and you're still the rookie cop. This is the only way to get the answers we need. I've got to do this."

In any case, she was wearing a ballistic vest under her clothes and had her gun holstered under her arm.

"Let me come with you. I could just be in the bar, you know, pretending to wait for my girlfriend."

"He knows what you look like Rick. Just accept it or I'm pulling rank."

Rick was beaten and he knew it. He hadn't known Gamby long, but he had seen that look before and knew when her mind was set.

"Across the street with Jeremy. If anything happens-"

"I'll call. Don't worry."

Gamby picked up her coat and took one final look at her desk. Hopefully this little meeting wouldn't end up costing her her job.

"Oh and if you get bored you could always play a game with Jeremy, but be careful."

Rick raised an eyebrow.

"He cheats."

49

When Eddie reached the headquarters of The Circle he wasn't really aware of the heavy sports bag he was carrying. The members at the door just greeted him like they had always done, assuming he was there to do his regular cleaning duties. Even members in the Seventh Circle had menial chores to do. It kept operating costs down. It wasn't until he stepped inside the broom closet that he noticed the bag. Where had it come from? He opened it and looked inside. The axe was there, dried blood still on the blade. His eyes lost their focus for a moment. His brain blazed red hot and then everything became clear. He knew why he took it. There was work to be done here as well. The most important work. The work that would change everything. But not time yet.

He sat down in the closet and closed his eyes. He had hours to wait. Hours before the deed would be done. In the darkness of the broom closet he sat and listened to the little voice inside his head, promising everything. He smiled as it whispered to him of his hopes and dreams made real.

50

"So I'm here. Where's your back-up?"

Gamby didn't even notice him sitting next to her in the bar. The place was so crowded and noisy. Saturdays were always worse than Fridays. She had to take a second look just to make sure it was him.

"You shaved your head."

"That's right."

"And you're growing a beard."

"Well, that's just laziness."

What was she doing there? She felt completely out of her league. This man was a killer, of some sort. She was probably making a big mistake. Rick was just a call away, all she had to do was-

"I'll have a dark rum. Single. What about you?"

"Ah. Beer, please."

The bartender went off to get their drinks. Camper didn't look half as nervous as he should have been. He almost looked resigned.

"Why are you here?"

"That was going to be my question."

The bartender laid a beer on the counter in front of her

and a glass of dark rum next to Camper.

"This is a crazy world."

He took a sip of his drink. She decided to start.

"Is it true you're a priest?"

That was abrupt. The bartender gave them each a look and went to tend the rest of the counter. Camper almost choked on his drink. He shouldn't have been surprised. The way things were going, nothing should be surprising to him anymore.

"Who told you that?"

"Jeremy Daniels."

"I don't know anyone named Jeremy."

She put the beer to her mouth. Already on the ropes. That was good. He has no idea how much you know. Keep him off-balance until he slips.

"Are you going to arrest me?"

"Not yet. How much do you know about the Society for the Recognition of Meta-States?"

She's starting slow. Good. Now to give her something she doesn't know.

"I know their boss is lying dead in a secret basement under St. Pat's Church, along with one of his cronies."

She almost took out her gun then and there. Dr. Martin was dead? And in St. Pat's? That didn't make any sense. A secret basement? But they had been over the place with a fine toothed comb.

"Did you...?"

"Neither one of them, but thank you for asking. You might want to leave these ones alone. It would make for a very sloppy and very unsolved case file. I can have them taken care of if you like. Or maybe you don't want to hear about any of that?"

She didn't. If her career wasn't over yet, then it would be soon. She had to tread lightly. She had to remind herself that this was a dangerous man. So she decided to just ask him outright.

"Where were you the night Father Sal Detore was murdered?"

Camper took another sip of his rum and tapped on the counter in the direction of the bartender for another one.

"You already know the answer to that question, don't you?"

"I want to hear you say it."

Camper downed what he had left and pushed the empty glass away from him.

"Sal was the closest thing in this world I had to a friend. Do you know he used to be a missionary? Of course you do. You probably know more about him than I do. He was a good man. And he deserved way better than he got."

The bartender returned and put another glass in front of Camper and Gamby found herself relaxing for the first time all evening. She could feel his remorse. It was almost tangible. And more importantly, it was honest. She had met sad people before, guilty people. It came with the badge, but at that moment Camper King seemed the saddest person she had ever met in her life. She had this sudden urge to put her arm around him and tell him that everything would be okay. Instead, she raised her hand to the bartender and ordered two more beer. There was a two for one special, after all.

When the door to her apartment finally opened, Rick jumped to his feet. It had been three hours and he was scared to death. Jeremy had produced a Scrabble board from somewhere and they were stuck debating whether *decandency* was an actual word when Gamby and Camper walked in. Well, stumbled in was more like it. Stumbled in singing *Bat Out of Hell*. Rick was incredulous.

"Where have you been? Do you know what time it is? And you're drunk!"

Camper was holding her up under one arm and leaning on her at the same time. Somehow he noticed Jeremy with his hazy eyes.

"What the hell are you doing here, you crazy monkey?"

For once Jeremy was gracious and helped Camper to the couch. Gamby's apartment was small, but they managed to find room for everybody. Rick insisted on staying and hauled a few cushions off the couch to sleep on. After encouraging her to drink two full glasses of water, he helped Gamby to bed and then helped Jeremy sort out Camper. They gave him the floor since it was easy for him in his condition to sleep anywhere.

"Salacious. You think I don't remember but I do."

Camper rolled over. He was a mess, but maybe he needed it.

"It's all been coming back to me. All of it. In little bits and pieces, but it's still coming back."

Jeremy gave him a weary look as Rick brought Camper a blanket. He had done things with The Circle. Things he wouldn't like the others to know. It was a fragile alliance they had formed and it had been going smoothly so far. Camper could ruin it all with a few drunken remarks.

"Go to sleep Camper."

But Camper had already nodded off, fully clothed and in a position that would make his back ache in the morning once the alcohol wore off. Jeremy smiled and thought about the look that would be on his face the next day. He was looking forward to King's embarrassment.

The morning came swiftly and Rick was up before any of them, making tea and toasting bread. He hadn't really slept the night, instead opting to listen to every little noise that the apartment made and thinking on what they could be. He got his second wind at about eight thirty in the morning and started cleaning the kitchen. He'd certainly crash later, but he was feeling alright now. He had also done the unthinkable and switched off all the phones in the house. He had convinced himself it was a good idea in the very wee hours. That way everybody could have a good sleep and not be disturbed. As a cop fresh out of the academy switching off *anything* belonging to a detective was taboo, but something told him it made sense. He couldn't really explain it.

Later that morning when the whole bleary-eyed crew turned on Gamby's little black and white Hitachi, both of its only channels were broadcasting the same story.

The largest mass murder to occur in the city in forty years happened last night in a compound on the outskirts of the city. The scene was described as grizzly by the delivery man who reported the crime around six o'clock this morning.

Gamby went for her phone instinctively and found it turned off. Rick didn't say a word. Camper chalked it up to her being loaded that night. And in the meantime Jeremy's eyes were locked on the television.

Reports indicate that the compound was the site of a cult

organization. As of yet we do not have any details on just how many people were killed or what kind of cult it was, but we will continue to update you on this story as the day progresses.

In a related story, Vanessa Gamby, lead detective in the Pentagram Killer investigation , has been reported as missing. Anyone with information regarding her whereabouts is asked to contact the City Police Headquarters.

A picture of Gamby appeared on screen and Gamby winced. She always hated herself in pictures.

Police would also like to ask for any information regarding this man -

The all too familiar 'Frenchie the sketch artist' rendering of Camper with hair flashed up next.

- known as Camper King. King is wanted for questioning by the police.

Rick turned off the television. Gamby just sat there, shaking her head.

"What am I doing? I must be completely insane."

Rick was thinking a little more rational.

"Why did they report you as missing? I don't get it."

"Why? Besides the fact that my phone is never turned off? I'm the lead investigator in the case of a serial killer. And last night there's a mass murder. The first thing they'd do is call me. No one tells the police to wait forty eight hours. Especially for one of their own."

Rick still didn't buy it.

"But no one came to the apartment looking for you. It doesn't make sense."

"None of this makes sense, Rick. We're dealing with things far beyond the realm of sense."

Jeremy was still staring at the screen, dumbfounded.

He hadn't said anything. Hadn't even moved. Camper had expected at least one sarcastic remark from him this morning, but none were forthcoming. What was wrong with him?

"Hey Salacious? What is it?"

Gamby threw Camper a look.

"It's Jeremy, Camper, he likes to be called Jeremy."

"Someone hit The Circle."

"Yeah. It looks that way."

"They're all dead."

"We don't know that for sure."

"First those college kids. Now the rest. Some of them had a future. Some of them were young enough that they could get out. Half of our members are just there to rebel against their parents. It's a phase. They grow out of it and leave. We let them go. For the ones that are serious, leaving is harder. The more secrets you're told, the tighter the grip becomes, but there were people there who didn't deserve to die."

Camper couldn't believe the words coming out of his mouth were his own.

"I'll get to the bottom of it. Don't worry."

Jeremy actually took some comfort from that. Even if he suspected that there was nothing Camper would be able to do, it was nice to hear. If someone had launched an assault on The Circle it meant only one thing. Someone was after the Charter. And they probably had it already.

The thought had already occurred to Camper and in a way he was thankful. The only reason anyone would want the Charter would be to destroy it and he had tried to do it himself years ago if he remembered right. And his memories were jumbled at best. Maybe this would finally free him.

"They were after the Charter, weren't they?" Rick was asking Camper, but it was Jeremy who answered.

"If they got it, we're in mounds of trouble."

"What do you mean? Shouldn't that be the end of it?"

"It'll be worse. Much worse. The whole city will suffer."

Gamby was already dealing with a headache from the night before. She didn't need another one, but it didn't look like anyone else was going to ask.

"Why, Jeremy? What will happen? I thought you said that whoever takes it will just end up with a target on their back."

"There's more to it. Worst case scenario the city will go up in flames. At best The Dot's economy will take a long walk on a very short pier. People will lose their homes and businesses. Suicides. Looting. The National Guard gets called in and this place ends up a ghost town.

"I don't get it. Why would that happen?"

"Because the Charter was a deal between *the city itself* and the Devil. The men who signed it got their fair share and then they died, but they signed it as representatives of the City. That's why the place is prosperous. That's why people still move here and raise their families and open stores and restaurants. The moment the Charter is gone, who knows what will happen. Didn't know about that when you went for it, did you King?"

"No. I didn't. At least, I don't think I did."

Gamby quickly grabbed her coat and headed for the door. Rick stood between, holding a plate of toast.

"Where are you going?"

"I'm going to bite the bullet and go to work. It's the only way we're going to find out if the Charter has been taken."

"What happens when they ask where you've been?"

"I'll lie. Jermey and Camper, you stay here. I don't want you out there making my job harder. I'll call if I find out something. Rick, you coming?"

Rick had already taken the plate back to the kitchen and was getting his own coat. Gamby turned to Jeremy and Camper.

"Try not to kill each other okay?"

They grinned.

"Does this mean you believe me? You're not going to turn me in?"

Gamby was already half way out the door when she heard Camper and turned back for a moment.

"Let's just say I'm not the same person I was yesterday."

"That's good enough for me."

Jeremy munched on a slice of toast.

"Looks like it's just us, King. So tell me, do you play Scrabble?"

51

Six hours had passed since Eddie had stepped into the broom closet, clutching his gym bag with the axe inside. The voice in the back of his head had kept him company, whispering promises and dreams. Anything he wanted would be his. All he had to do was one little task. The simplest of things.

A voice from the hallway woke him out of his trance. It was Voracious. He must have been talking on a cell phone.

"No. I don't want to hear it. I want everything connecting those kids with The Circle destroyed...well I don't know. You're the Chief of Police, you figure it out...No, I've never spoken to them, but all three were supposed to be working here tonight...Reggie, there are no coincidences. We're having it moved. Just in case...Not over the phone."

Voracious hung up and started walking away from the closet. The whispering voice told Eddie that this was the right moment. If he didn't act now, the chance would be gone.

Without warning Voracious felt a sharp pain in the

back of his leg. He let out a yell and fell to the floor. As he turned himself around to see what had happened Eddie was raising his axe for another blow.

"All you have to do is tell me where. That's it. Tell me where and the Great One will let you live."

Voracious remembered the young man. Recently initiated into the Seventh Circle. His father had killed himself years ago. Was this some sort of pay back?

"Look. I really don't know what you're talking about. We can settle this. Anything you want."

For a split second it looked like Eddie was trying to decide, but it really wasn't a contest. What could he provide that the Great One himself couldn't? He raised his axe high above his head.

"Where is it?"

Malicious saw the whole terrible interview from just around the corner. Voracious lost his right leg to the axe and then he started spilling his guts. He left nothing out. Four of the five w's. Plus the how. When and where the Charter was being moved. Who was guarding it. And how it was getting there.

Once he had learned everything he needed, Eddie let his axe drop, splitting open Voracious' chest cavity. Malicious held back the bile gathering in his throat and wasted no time in fleeing the compound. He had the center chair now, in fact, the only chair. If something were to happen to the Charter he'd be the one to blame. Any favors he had left, he had to call them in now. And there wasn't much time.

52

When Gamby and Rick arrived on the scene it was already well under control, officers and CSI's were combing the wooded areas behind the compound. There were ambulances lining the street in front of the building, as well as cop cars and some media vans. Rick went to one of the cars to get the latest as Gamby approached the door. A tall cop named Dawson was on guard.

"I wouldn't go in there Detective."

"What's wrong Dawson?"

A voice came yelling from inside.

"Is that Gamby?! Get in here!"

Dawson gave her a look as if he'd been listening to that same yell all day.

"That's what's wrong."

"What's the Chief doing here?"

"I think some of the victims were connected. Sons of politicians maybe. He's furious."

"I'll keep it in mind."

"Good luck."

"Thanks."

She was going to need all the luck she could muster to

get through the day with her job still intact. Well at least the city wasn't in flames yet, but maybe that was just a matter of time.

"Gamby!"

Reggie Law - no pun intended - looked every bit the cliché police chief. A tad on the heavy side, he loved smoking cigars and barking at cops in his office. He even had a fishing trophy hung over his desk. He loved to talk about that fish. She'd been trapped in his office more than once hearing the story. Gamby always felt that there was something not quite right about him, but working for the police in The Dot did things to people. Even though the pay was good no one stayed around for too long. Gamby was an exception, as well as a few others, including the Chief. In fact he'd been there for twenty years and eight of those as Chief of Police.

When Gamby walked in she could smell the bodies. They were in random places as if cut down while they were walking, or sitting or just going about their business. And everywhere was the blood. The Chief was leaning over one corpse in particular, an unlit cigar hanging from his mouth. The body was missing a leg and his chest had been hacked away. She didn't need any of the lab boys to tell her what had happened. She had seen something like it already.

"Where've you been?"

"My mother. She was sick. I had to leave right away, but I left my phone charger here. Once I got to her, I didn't think to call. I just got back this morning."

Chief Reggie gave her a once over and then grunted and turned back to the body. It looked like he bought it. That was good. She hadn't worked on the story long and God help her if her mother showed up in town for a surprise visit.

"So, what do we have here Chief?"

The Chief pushed his cigar to the side of his mouth and absently checked the body on the floor.

"A mess. A big fucking mess, Gamby. That's what we've got here. I've never seen anything like it. The paperwork alone is going to take weeks."

"Do we have any suspects?"

"Well, what about yours? Camper King? He's been on our wanted list since the murder at St. Pat's. Now we've got a building full of dead Satanists. Seems to fit somehow."

"No. There's no way."

Gamby stopped herself and the Chief gave her a look. She quickly covered her tracks.

"The serial killer, if it is King, wouldn't be interested in killing Satanists. The robe we recovered from the taxi driver, the one King was wearing the night the priest was killed, the victims here are wearing the same robes. He was probably one of them."

The Chief nodded slowly.

"Maybe a falling out. Or maybe you're right. Although the idea of a serial killer and a mass murderer out there on the loose at the same time isn't a nice thought, is it?"

"No sir."

He stood up and straightened his beaten coat.

"See what you can do here. I know you've got your hands full already, but you're my best. Bring in anyone you need. I'll warn you. Some of these men were on the City Council. The Head of Sanitation is in the room down the hall. And Governor Rice's son is decapitated and lying near the back door. That's going to cause a headache. Might even cost a few jobs before it's all over. So take it easy, alright?"

"I will."

She started to breathe a little sigh of relief.

"Just let the lab boys do what they do best and take it one step at a time. It's gonna be a lot of work so don't rush."

"Thanks Chief."

"I hope your mother is feeling better."

He left her alone there, standing over one of the many bodies in the place. Some of the CSI's were just coming down the hall. Suddenly overwhelmed by the scene, Gamby left the building for a deep breath of air. Early retirement was looking better and better all the time.

53

Jeremy and Camper were just considering dinner – with an eye to some leftovers labeled *puttanesca* - when the telephone rang. They both froze. Since each of them were wanted by the police, answering a detective's home telephone didn't seem like the best idea. Camper was the first to move.

"It's probably her anyway. Hello?"

It was Michael on the other end.

"What are you doing answering the phone? You're wanted by the police!"

"Michael, how did you know I was here?"

"I followed you last night. Somebody has to watch your back. But I didn't expect you to get her drunk and go back to her place. You're crazy."

"It's not like that. Why are you calling?"

"I guess you haven't been watching the news."

"What's happened?"

"Someone's burned down St. Pat's."

Camper just stood there for a moment, holding the phone, dumbstruck. Jeremy mouthed the words *what's wrong*.

"When did it happen?"

"This morning I think. So I guess you'll be needing a cab, then?"

Yeah. He'd be needing a cab alright. And a stiff drink. And someone to punch. Hard.

"Better wait until it gets dark, Michael."

Camper hung up the phone. He had no idea who would have done it. Aside from Michael, Gamby and himself, everyone who knew about St. Pat's was dead. Or in Rome. The possibilities were frightening.

Jeremy had just popped a tupperware container in the microwave.

"So what's happening?"

"We're going out tonight, honey. Call the sitter."

54

Malicious Black wasn't a coward, but he knew better than to stick around when an axe-wielding homicidal maniac was killing everyone in sight. He had sworn to protect the Charter. And that's just what he planned to do. Unlike *Albert,* he had balls. He'd grown up on the street and had worked his way up through the group since he was fifteen. Voracious' father might have been a powerful man, but he died just like the rest of them. Malicious had to think fast. He knew the Charter was being moved. This place wasn't safe anymore. And Salacious was still out there. Or was he? Something else Voracious was supposed to have taken care of. Some center chair he turned out to be. Once again Malicious had to take care of everything himself.

He ditched his robes on the way out and took out his cell phone. He knew a guy who was good with things like this. As much as he would have liked to deal with Salacious personally, the Charter was priority. It always had been and always would be. No matter what was going to happen, he'd remain loyal to The Circle.

The phone stopped ringing just as Malicious was

making his way through the wooded area behind the compound. An automated voice messaging system cut in.

"Hello. You've reached Handsome Laundry. Please leave a message and we'll get right back to you. And have a nifty day."

Malicious took a breath, spoke the words *Salacious Cain,* and hung up. The deed was done. No going back now. He had officially put a hit out on the former leader of The Circle. But with Voracious gone, he was the leader now. And if there would be any blame dished out, he'd be the one strapping on a bib and eating buffet.

Next was the Charter. It was probably already on the move, unless Voracious had shirked that responsibility too, but there was no way he was going back to the compound to check. Once he got to the road he feigned an injury and flagged down a car. The little old lady inside didn't appreciate being hauled out and left in the dust. He had taken the name Malicious for a reason.

55

Gamby made her way through the compound, trying to take the whole scene in at once. The television had gotten it right. It was grizzly. Grizzly bear grizzly. Rick was doing better at this scene than the last. He hadn't touched anything. She suspected he was just trying not to throw up. None of the other cops gave him a second look. Rumor had gone around that Rick was in *training*. Whatever that meant. She hadn't started the rumor, but it made things easier having him there.

"So what do we think?"

Gamby was leaning over the body of a teenager. He'd been almost hacked in two.

"I think this is sick."

"Same guy who did those Circle kids a few days ago?"

"Has to be. They've been killed in the same way."

Rick lowered his voice.

"What about the Charter? You think it's still here?"

"Only one way to find out."

Gamby took out her cell phone. Not that she really expected Jeremy to pick up, but it was worth a shot.

"Hello?"

"Jeremy, what are you doing answering the phone?"

"Ah. Well. Aren't you glad I did?"

She could hear Camper in the background snickering. What were they up to?

"Jeremy, where's the Charter? We need to check to see if it's still here."

Jeremy suddenly straightened up. He was about to reveal a secret he'd sworn to keep. A secret he had shed blood over. Nothing good could come of it.

"You'll have to go to my office."

"Your office?"

"What used to be my office. It's a little room, just off the Library of the Three."

"Library of the Three?"

"Yeah, I know."

Gamby and Rick followed Jeremy's instructions until they found themselves in a small office. On the wall was a detailed print of Bosch's *The Garden of Earthly Delights*. They removed the print from the wall revealing a safe behind it. Gamby was shocked.

"You store the Charter in here? I've got a better safe at home and all that's inside is some jewelry."

"No. Of course not. In the safe is a key. The key leads to the room where the Charter is kept."

"Okay, that makes a little more sense. What's the combination?"

"I can't believe I'm telling you this."

"Come on Jeremy. We don't have much time."

"One two three. Three two one. Six six six. There you go."

Gamby shook her head and got started on the safe. A few button pushes later, the door swung open. Inside were a few issues of Ninja magazine, a collection of Doors tapes and five thousand dollars in cash, but no key.

"It would have been small and gold plated. Are you sure it's not there?"

"Jeremy, where's the room it's supposed to be in?"

"You know I'm asking for it just by telling you this. Someone's going to get me. I know it."

"I'm going to get you if you don't tell me. Don't forget what's at stake here."

He relented and, following Jeremy's directions, Gamby and Rick made their way to a small kitchen. Inside they found two members of the cult, bloody and hacked up. One of them had been in the process of making a ham and cheese sandwich. The refrigerator had been pushed to the side revealing an open door and a long set of stairs. Gamby was still on her phone with the former cult leader.

"Okay. These stairs go down. Is there anything we should expect?"

"Are you talking about booby traps?"

"Well. I don't know. A security system, maybe?"

"Satan himself created The Circle to hide and keep the Charter. It never needed security before."

Gamby and Rick started walking down the stairs. It wasn't long. She felt they had maybe gone down two stories. The stairs ended with a simple wooden door, this one open as well. Inside was a plain white room like a just finished basement apartment. In the center of the room was a gold plated podium. And on the podium -

"Is it still there?"

Jeremy was getting anxious.

"No. It's gone. There's nothing here, Jeremy. Just a white room and an empty podium."

Rick had been examining the door to the room. He could tell Gamby was nearing the end of her patience. She was known for her quick temper around the station. Especially when hitting a dead end. This particular dead end might end up being that certain straw placed on that special camel's hump. He gave her his best smile.

"Well, the city isn't on fire."

Gamby gave him a look, but he wasn't about to let up.

"If whoever killed everyone here took the Charter and planned on destroying it, don't you think they would have done it by now? Plenty of time has gone by since it was taken, more than enough to do the deed. I mean, it's just a piece of paper and all you need is a Bic."

Gamby knew he was right. If things were supposed to get bad, they would have by now. Maybe there was another explanation.

"I'll call you back, Jeremy."

Before he could respond, she had hung up and was slowly circling the room, letting her mind think of every possible angle. And then it hit her like divine lightening.

"It's been moved."

"Huh?"

"It's had to have been moved. The killer was too late. He came down here and found exactly what we found, nothing."

"Why would it be moved? If they knew this was coming, wouldn't they have tried to protect themselves?

The guy upstairs with the ham and cheese sandwich certainly didn't know about this."

She turned it over in her head, but it didn't take long. And it made so much sense.

"Jeremy."

"Jeremy?"

Gamby nodded. That had to be it.

"He left The Circle. And he was their leader, privy to all their secrets. They moved it because he was a security leak. That's why it's not here. No one stole it. It was brought to a more secure location."

She knew it was true even as she said it. Now it was just a matter of finding out where it had been moved. And maybe Jeremy could help out with that too. She reached for her phone.

"Vanessa? If Jeremy was a security leak, wouldn't you think they'd send someone after him?"

The realization hit her like a brick and she hit speed dial on her phone while they ran out of the compound and toward her car.

But line was busy.

56

The Handsome Laundry Shop on East Street was anything but handsome. It was a dirty little square building that looked ready to fall down: bricks hanging off the walls in places and its windows sad eyes covered in grime. It was the last place one would expect to find a laundromat. And even more surprising to see a devilishly well-dressed man, immaculately groomed and carrying a plastic covered suit over his shoulder, exit from the rotting back door. He turned to lock the door and tapped some dust from his polished shoes. As he walked away from the building he began to whistle. And his whistle turned into a song.

"The handsome laundry man, the handsome laundry man, doing the best that I can, 'cause I'm the handsome laundry man."

He continued the song all the way down the block, smiling at the sky and even doing a little dance as he made his way around a fire hydrant. No one gave him a second look, not even the dogs. The locals all knew what he did for a living and it had nothing to do with laundry. He had made sure they knew. A little gentle persuasion had kept the locals in check for years. Nobody wanted another killing in their neighborhood, so they left him alone and nobody died. Pretty simple really. And if anyone made trouble for the street he took care of it. Aside from that first murder it was actually a good deal. The Handsome Laundry Shop might have been dilapidated, but the rest of the neighborhood used to be worse: crack dens, gang turf, prostitutes. He had run them all off on his own. But that first murder - he hated that word, it sounded so evil - that was the reason no one looked him in the eye. That was what had given him the power.

He stopped into a local store and got himself a newspaper. He never paid for anything at the local. The headlines were all Pentagram Killer Strikes Again and Pentagram Killer on the Loose. He didn't really care. It was his turn to step up to the plate and he was more than ready.

He put up his hand to hail a cab. Cabbies had lately started to go through this part of town. It might have been sketchy, but roadwork had made it a detour for months. A cab pulled up and he handed the driver a piece of paper with some directions written on it. His next job was Salacious Cain. And he already knew exactly where to start.

57

Michael pulled up to the apartment block fifteen minutes late. He didn't like it, but he thought that he should prepare first. And that meant eating. In fact he was still eating when Camper hopped into the front seat.

"Glad to see you had time to stop for a cheeseburger."

"Better safe than sorry. Who's this?"

Jeremy had gotten into the back seat. He was wearing his hospital gown under his jacket. He said it was slimming.

"Michael this is Salacio- Jeremy. Jeremy Daniels."

Michael turned in his seat and gave Jeremy a once over.

"Well doesn't that take the ice-cream cake."

"What? Is there a problem?"

Michael took another bite of his cheeseburger and started to pull away from the curb.

"I never expected to have the former head of a Satanic Order and a rouge Vatican Agent in my cab at once. That's all."

Jeremy's eyes went wide.

"How did you -"

"Don't worry. Your secret is safe. Let's just say I've been around and leave it at that, okay?"

"King, do you trust this guy?"

Camper choked for a second. This was not the Salacious Cain he remembered dealing with.

"He saved my life."

"Well. That's good. Nice to meet you, Michael."

He nodded to Michael in the rearview mirror and Michael returned the gesture. This was definitely not the same person Camper remembered punching in the face.

Just as they turned off of Gamby's street it started to rain. Not just a few drops either. It poured like someone had left the firmament running. Camper and Jeremy gave each other a look.

"This can't be it."

"I don't think it is."

Michael was lost.

"Can't be what?"

"You tell him."

"No. I'm not going through it again."

"Well, *I* don't want to."

Michael stopped the car. The rain continued to pour down in bathtubs and he half expected rubber ducks to start hitting the windshield.

"Somebody better tell me what's going on, or you're both gonna to get very wet on the way back to the detective's apartment."

Camper took a deep breath and started to speak. A half hour and a game of twenty questions later the rain had gone from bathtub to shower-stall.

"So you thought this sudden torrential downpour was

a sign of the city's imminent destruction because a pact with the devil had gone sour?"

Jeremy and Camper gave each other a look.

"Yeah that's about it."

"That's what I thought anyway."

Michael started the cab and pulled away from the curb.

"I've seen some crazies in this taxi, but you two are the absolute nuttiest. Don't get me wrong, I know some of the things you guys are into *actually* exist. I'm pretty supernatural myself, but the city signing a deal with the devil? I have to see that one to believe it."

Jeremy shifted uncomfortably in the back seat. It felt like the statue of Mary on the dash was staring at him. It bobbed back and forth like a mini hula dancer, chastising all his life choices.

"How much longer until we get there?"

"Just around this corner. Holy shit!"

Out of nowhere a man in a dark suit walked in front of the cab. Michael pulled a hard right and started hydroplaning out of control and they crashed head first into a willing telephone pole. Airbags exploded open and everything went black for the three amigos. The rain continued to drizzle down and the man in the dark suit casually walked away from the slowly steaming cab.

58

Rick had been hitting redial on Gamby's phone while they drove over the speed limit toward her apartment. She was worried about Jeremy; nothing to do with the fact that if he was killed in her apartment she'd probably end up off the force and in prison. Nothing at all. Strange as it was, she really was genuinely worried.

"Anything yet?"

"Nothing. No one's picking up. Maybe they went out?"

"Yeah. They went out."

Gamby sped through a red light. She had told them to stay put. If they were out...But her gut was telling her otherwise. No. They were in trouble. She had to get home.

"Um. Vanessa?"

"What is it Rick?"

"You're doing a hundred and ten."

Gamby took a double take at the speedometer and followed that with a calming breath. She forced her foot to relax and take it down. No good killing someone along the way. Especially the way the rain was hitting the pavement.

She hadn't seen anything like it before. Not in all her years in The Dot. And not in Shepherd's Grove either.

"Can you still see?"

He was right. The rain was getting so hard that her wipers could barely keep up.

"Maybe we should pull over. Wait for it to calm down."

But what if it didn't calm down? What if this was it? The whole city washed away in one day. Like Atlantis. People would come from all over just to see where the city used to be. If this was it, maybe they were too late.

"Vanessa, don't you think we should pull over? I can't see through my side of the windshield. I don't know how you are."

Gamby's senses returned. Thank God for Rick and his dumb voice. She immediately took the thought back. No. Not dumb. He was probably the smartest one out of all of them. She flicked her indicator and pulled over to where she believed the curb to be. A slight thud when she stopped told her she had put a wheel on the sidewalk. Good enough. At least she wouldn't be knocking anyone down.

They sat there like that in the rain for twenty minutes, neither really sure what to say. Gamby didn't want to talk about the case, and neither did Rick. For twenty minutes it didn't seem to matter. They were in Limbo. Capable of nothing.

"Where are you from, Rick?"

Rick gave her a look as if it was the weirdest question he'd ever been asked.

"You don't know?"

"No. Should I?"

"Everyone at headquarters knows."

"Well I don't. Where are you from?"

"Canada."

"What?"

"My father's from Detroit. Mom's from Ottawa. I moved here seven years ago, took the pledge and the rest is history."

"I thought you sounded a little funny."

Rick was looking out the window.

"Rain's let up. We better get back on the road."

Gamby's mind switched gears immediately and she started the engine.

"Keep trying the phone. We'll be there in five minutes."

59

Malicious was just a boy when his father had brought him into The Circle. He felt so proud sharing the secret with his Dad. This huge secret underneath everything. Not even his mother knew about it. It was their little pact. Father and son. It had made him feel so special.

And when Malicious had reached the Third Circle his father's face was beaming. All the secrets were told then. All the terrible and dirty parts. About their real purpose serving the Great One. About the Charter. He had been prepared of course. Tutored and instructed. Given half truths and pieces. But when he had finally been led to the room and told the story, he had actually started to cry. It was so perfect.

"Malicious. It's time for me to go."

Malicious had been initiated into the Second Circle not long ago and his father stood before him. They didn't call each other father and son in The Circle. They were both servants to a higher being and such titles were meaningless.

"I understand."

The old man –he had become so old these past few

years- put his hand on Malicious' shoulder.

"I'd like you to be there."

"Of course I will. It's my duty."

His father lowered his voice.

"You don't have to be the one. There are others you know. Others who could do it."

Malicious clenched his teeth.

"I know. But I will. It's my responsibility."

There was a look of sad resignation, just for a moment, in the old man's eyes. He couldn't be weak now. He had to be strong. Strong for his son. He had been ready for this for thirty years. Thirty years of serving and now the end. He had to be strong.

They led him to a small room and placed him on a wooden altar. The rest of the First Circle were there, as well as the second. They began chanting as soon as he was placed on the altar. Slow at first. And quiet. Someone handed Malicious a knife. The chanting rose and rose. He held it above his head, gave his father one last look, and plunged deep.

The memory faded and Malicious ditched his stolen car. He was just outside the city now. Far from any prying eyes. The trail in the woods was intact. None of their failsafe measures had been compromised. It was just a twenty minute hike through the woods to the Charter's second home and he hoped it was still there. Voracious might have spilled the Satanic beans, but Malicious had a head start. And he knew how to get in.

60

"I can't believe it's gone."

They stood there- Michael, Salacious and Camper – in the cold drizzle and just stared. The Church had been reduced to ashes and rock in one night. Nothing was left. Camper stepped past the obligatory yellow tape for everyone's protection. There was no one else out on the street. The rain had taken care of that. Michael and Salacious followed Camper through the rubble. It had to be there. It had to be. But he knew deep down that it was the only reason for anyone to burn down the church. To get rid of it. All of it.

"What are you looking for, Camper?"

But who? Who would want to do it? Had the Vatican decided finally to cut him off? Destroying all the evidence of what he had done would certainly do that. But burning down a church was definitely not their style. Especially when they could have just shredded the documents like any other corporate cover-up. Then who?

"Camper?"

Camper was picking through the rubble.

"Camper?"

"Hold on a second. I need to think."

He was being manipulated. He knew that. The Hanged Man had an altar under the Church. Maybe that was the target. Pieces started to fall into place. The war in Hell. Evil versus evil. The Hanged Man had a one up on the others. So somebody decided to take care of it. To destroy the place of possession. It made perfect sense, in a very evil sort of way.

"Jeremy. Did you know what was hidden under this Church?"

"Yeah I knew. The place where the Charter was signed."

"Also an altar to the Hanged Man."

Michael was having that lost feeling again.

"Who?"

Finally, Jeremy was in his element.

"The Hanged Man. One of the greater demons of Hell."

"One of the ones in the Charter?"

"That's right. The Hanged Man. A Thousand Needles. And The Lord of Worms."

Camper picked up a piece of brick and gave it a toss.

"So which one. Which one do you think did it?"

Jeremy thought. Of course. Destroying the Hanged Man's place of possession would diminish his influence, bringing the other two closer to victory. And then there was the voice from the hospital. The voice that had told him they wanted Camper back. The voice that had told him to kill Gamby. It wasn't even something he could consider now. She was kinda cute. Suddenly it hit him.

"The Hell Hound."

The others gave the universal sign for *what the hell are you talking about.*

"The Hell Hound. The one that attacked you at Phil's."

Camper wasn't sure.

"We don't even know if it was after me."

"Of course it was. I mean, how could it not be?"

Salacious had a point.

Michael was still lost.

"So a Hell Hound burned down the Church?"

"No. The Hell Hound is dead. I think whoever sent it burned down the church."

Camper's eyes widened.

"Hell Hounds are called Satan's dogs. Not just any demon, no matter how great, can let one loose in the world."

"That's exactly what I'm saying. You've been turning the tide in the war. Helping out one side. Disturbing the balance. I think the Great One himself wants you out of the equation. He sent the Hell Hound. You took care of it. So next he burns down the Hanged Man's place of possession. He knows it's probably just a matter of time before the balance is disturbed again. So the next logical step would be-"

Jeremy stopped suddenly. It couldn't be. But it all made sense. To call it all off. To end it. Maybe even start over somewhere else. And why not?

Michael was impatient, but Camper had already figured it out.

"What? What's the next step?"

Camper was already running back to the cab.

"He'll destroy the Charter."

61

When Gamby and Rick reached her apartment there was a message spelled out on the floor with Scrabble letters.

Be back soon.

Gamby was livid.

"Be back soon?! Be back soon!? Demons are on the loose and the city is about to blow up and they leave a note that says *be back soon*?"

"Maybe they just went to the store?"

"A Satanist and a Vatican agent both wanted by the police just went to the store? Yeah. Maybe they wanted to get some Pez."

"Star Wars Pez."

"You're not helping Rick."

"Well at least we know they went out on their own. They weren't taken or killed."

"That's making me feel a whole lot better."

"Where do you think they went?"

Gamby didn't have time to respond. The knife came out of nowhere, coming straight out of Rick's stomach. He let out a sick moan. His eyes were pleading. This can't be happening. This isn't supposed to happen. She had her gun out in a half second and let off ten shots before Rick hit the floor. The man behind him, the smart dressed owner of the Handsome Laundry, fell back against the wall, bleeding from his chest.

"Rick!"

But he was already dead. They both were. She sat on the floor next to Rick and tried to put herself back together. Everything was crazy now. She'd completely lost control. Camper and Jeremy were gone. The Charter was missing. And now Rick was dead. She had never really been close to any of the other officers. But they were becoming friends. Watson and Holmes in a damned city. But in those stories it was Holmes that finally died, not Watson.

She held his head in her lap and cried as the rain started again.

62

Phil was restocking the canned goods shelf when the door opened. With everything that had happened recently he was glad for the business. But when he walked behind the counter he saw someone he didn't expect.

"Where are your chips?"

"Second aisle."

He recognized Malicious Cain immediately. The man who had caught him when he went searching for the city charter. His was one of the faces burned in his memory. He turned his back and pretended to take stock of the cigarettes on the wall, praying that he hadn't been recognized.

"Do you have any ketchup chips?"

"No. Sorry."

Malicious put a bag of sour cream and onion on the counter. He was carrying a briefcase. Phil wanted to know what was inside. Couldn't be good. He decided to seize the moment. He reached over to the other side of the register and grabbed a can of peas. Malicious didn't see it coming. And who would have? It's not everyday you get struck on the head by a tin can while buying a bag of chips in a corner store. Although given the store's recent history maybe he should have expected it. If he had known.

Phil turned the open sign to read *closed,* dimmed the lights and dragged the unconscious Satanist to the broom closet. Then he started working on forcing the briefcase open.

63

Eddie killed everyone at the site. There weren't many. Just a few guards posted around the shack. And one in the hidden basement. That was easy enough to find. The Circle weren't a tremendously smart group, despite their charge. *Former* charge, he reminded himself. Putting a trap door under a rug? Far too simple. The trap door revealed a stone staircase and, after that, a security door. The door required a password for entry. That was easy enough, with the voice in his head. Anything was possible with the voice in his head. But once inside? Nothing. Absolutely nothing. Once again he had been beaten to it. And all the killing for nothing. All the chase for nothing. He couldn't believe it was all happening. Shouldn't everything have worked out? The voice had made promises. Everything should be going his way. But it wasn't. He was called the Prince of Lies. Could this be one of them? Was it all a test? Eddie was lost and the voice was silent. Was it ever really there?

In that little empty room, his humanity started to creep back in. Little by little. And when that little piece called compassion fell in place he collapsed to the floor in agony. So much killing. He could barely stand it. He beat his hands against the floor until they were red.

Reeling in distress, Eddie reached for his phone and called his Dad. He needed help and he didn't know what else to do. Chuck wasn't interested in helping at first but as soon as Eddie mentioned where he was, he changed his tune. Eddie shouldn't have even known where the shack was. How did he find it? And what was he even doing there? Chuck knew most of what the shack was for, but he had never been there personally. It was an opportunity he wasn't going to miss.

"Dad?"

Chuck had pulled his beat up old car right to the door of the shack. No guards, no traps. Something wasn't right. Worst of all was the look on Eddie's face. He'd seen that look before. Whenever a willing sacrifice realized the truth at the last minute. That was the face looking up from the table.

"Get in."

They drove for a half hour before speaking. Chuck wasn't even sure where he was going, but he figured out of town was the smartest route, so he started heading for the freeway. Eddie had been crying most of the way. Chuck had never been what one might call a model parent. Give the boy his space. Let him work it out. Just be here. And then the crying stopped. And Eddie finally spoke. Suddenly he was the epitome of calm.

"Stop the car."

"Do you think that's a good idea?"

"You have to stop the car."

Chuck pulled onto the shoulder of the road. They were

just approaching the outskirts of town, near the overpass and the freeway north. It was getting dark now and the rain clouds were retreating. Chuck didn't know what any of this was about, but maybe this was a chance. A chance for both of them to move on with their lives. To forget every sin of the past.

"I have to get out."

"Sure. Sure, son. Get some air."

Eddie lifted the latch and stepped out of the car. The voice had spoken to him. Had calmed him down and had shown him the way. He circled the car to the driver's side. His father rolled down the window.

"Are you okay, Eddie?"

Eddie looked up at the sky.

"I'm going to give you the peace you've been looking for, Chuck. I'm going to end all the pain."

"What are you talking about?"

In the next second Eddie put his fist through Chuck's skull.

64

They converged on Gamby's apartment almost simultaneously. Phil had taken the stairs while Michael, Jermey and Camper the elevator. Inside was a mess. Gamby was lying on the couch, clutching her gun and shaking. Rick was dead on the floor, a wound in his stomach. Another body lay against the wall and floor, bullet holes in his chest. Gamby didn't even notice the others coming in. Camper was the first to speak.

"Vanessa?"

"They killed him. They killed Rick."

"This man here? He killed Rick?"

"Him. And whoever sent him. Someone's going to pay for this."

Phil had never seen a dead body before (dead Hell Hound, yes, but not dead body) and was noticeably nervous.

"I'm sorry about Rick."

"Forget it. He died in the line of duty."

Gamby sat up, wiping her face. She was grim. Resolute. An officer of the law. No, more than that. She was a solider in the war against darkness. And this was just another casualty.

"So what's next?"

"Well-"

Jeremy stepped forward.

"We've found the Charter. Well, Phil found the Charter. Stole it, actually."

"I mugged someone to get it."

He pulled a piece of rolled parchment out of his coat. They started to gather around it when Michael spoke.

"Maybe we should...I mean...there are two dead bodies here."

Camper started to remove something from his coat.

"I'll deal with it. Go into the bedroom and have a look at the Charter. I'll let you know when I'm done."

Gamby wasn't sure about the situation, but Jeremy reassured her.

"He is a priest, after all."

Gamby remembered their talk in the bar, when Camper had offered to take care of the victims at St. Pat's. Obviously he had a way. She just didn't want to know about it.

Phil, Jeremy, Michael, and Gamby went into the bedroom. As they closed the door Gamby could see Camper opening her windows. Jeremy noticed too.

"It's for the smell."

Camper took a small leather bundle from his inside coat pocket and unfolded it on the coffee table. He had done this a hundred times. He knew that. All those memories that had been wiped clean were slowly sinking in. This would be his first time knowing he wouldn't forget. Rick didn't deserve it, but there was no other way.

To protect Gamby and the rest. How could she explain it to the police? There would be questions and more questions and very few answers. And they'd all end up in jail.

He wiped the sweat from his forehead.

The procedure was simple. A ritualistic cremation. Instantaneous. It prevented reanimation of a corpse. But was also handy in simple disposal since it burned only the corpse and nothing else. Didn't always work though. There were rites and wards that prevented burning after death. And so he had other methods. It was those methods that tagged him as a serial killer.

He removed a piece of chalk from the leather bundle as well as some leaves and salt. He drew some symbols around the bodies where they lay, even if it meant on the wall, and placed the other ingredients accordingly. As an afterthought he said a prayer over Rick. He thought for a moment that they should examine the body of the man who had killed him. But when his eyes fell on his face he knew. He had a memory of seeing him before. A hit-man. No ties or allegiances. Someone just in it for the money. Better that he was burned. Camper began to speak.

The text was a mash of Babylonian, Latin and Hindi. Camper remained still as he spoke, his eyes closed tightly. A breeze from the open window ran past him. He opened his eyes just a crack to make sure everything was alright, and then it hit him. A searing blast of heat. The body of the former hit-man sprang upright, controlled by a blind puppeteer. And the voice that came from him was far from human.

"Camper. Camper King. The deal's off. I'm calling an end."

The body jerked back and forth with each syllable. A deranged mime on Absinthe and PCB.

"What deal?"

Camper could barely open his eyes. The voice filled his brain. He wondered if the others could hear what was going on.

"Don't play coy, Camper. I know you've got your brain back. I can't get it now, but rest assured it will be mine. And when it is-"

The last few words were cut off as the hit man's body finally burst into flame. Camper shut his eyes again, clenching his teeth and continued the ritual. Rick's body soon followed suit. Nothing but a pile of ashes and memories remained.

He took a deep breath and opened the door to the bedroom.

"Got a mini-vac?"

Phil volunteered for vacuuming, just to take his mind off of the Charter. For some reason it was easier vacuuming up the ashes of two dead bodies then reading over a document written in blood. Not for the last time he wondered what the hell he was doing there.

When Camper finished telling the others about the visitor, Phil spoke up.

"We've got to get out of here. We've got to get out of here now."

The others weren't sure.

"Think! This guy who killed Rick *knew* to come here. The Devil knows to come here. We have to leave. Find some place to hide."

Camper agreed.

"You're right. This place isn't safe right now. We've got to find somewhere else to hold up."

But Jeremy wasn't convinced.

"Until when? This is Satan we're talking about. He's not going to get bored looking for us. We're not going to be able to wait him out."

Gamby had no time for Jeremy. She was sure he was the hit-man's real target.

"Look, Jeremy, I'm sure Camper has a plan. You've got a plan don't you?"

"Of course I do. We just need a place that's safe for a bit. While I get it together. I just need a little time."

They all breathed a collective sigh of quasi-relief and started thinking of possible safe houses.

Camper thought hard on where they could go. It would have to be damn safe. For one thing, he didn't have a plan.

65

At this stage, Eddie could almost sense where it was. It was nothing like seeing it in his head. It was more like a sense of direction. Knowing intuitively which way to get to the exit in a movie theatre. Or where the bathroom is most likely to be in a mall. But he was also starting to sense other things. The voice in his head, which had been silent since he had killed his father, had given him this gift of sense. There were others near his prize. Others that could stop him. Maybe he needed help. But who would be worthy to do his master's bidding except himself? The voice inside him whispered. The dead. The dead would serve the living.

Eddie turned from the direction of his hunt. Turned his eyes elsewhere and reached out with his mind to find those resting places where he would raise his master's army.

The Peddleton Street Cemetery had the distinction of being the resting place of victims of the cholera epidemic, many of whom had been duped into false cures and false hopes. The Cemetery was an angry place, full of rage and sadness. It was everything Eddie was looking for.

As he started toward the cemetery he could still feel his goal in the back of his mind. It was moving now. Moving in another direction. It didn't matter. They could move it to the end of the Earth and he'd still find it. Every hour that went by he realized another truth about the world. And the most important truth of them all: everything was possible.

66

It was a tight squeeze in Micheal's cab. Camper took the front to give directions while Phil, Jeremy and Gamby sat in the back. Phil had refused to go back to the store, despite the risk. He said for his father's sake he had to see it through to the end. When they asked Camper exactly where they were going he didn't respond, just said *you'll see when we get there*. More than once Jeremy's arm accidentally brushed Gamby's leg. But she didn't really mind. All in all the trip to Camper's supposed safe house was like any other late night teenage cruise. Phil even joked about stopping for pizza and Michael almost did.

"I don't see why we didn't go to my place. It's safe. No one knows about it. I was able to keep it a secret from the Society and that's saying something."

Camper rolled down his window a little.

"It's not right. Not easy to defend. If it comes to it we need a place that's easier to defend."

"Sounds like you're expecting a siege."

"You better hope it doesn't turn into one. Turn right here."

They were in an industrial part of town, full of

warehouses and automated factories. Rubber bands, paper clips, urinal cakes, just about anything you could think of was probably stored or manufactured somewhere in the area. All part of the unnatural economic boom that had been permanently rising in The Dot.

"That's the building there."

They pulled up next to a typical warehouse. Big doors. Very few windows. Camper got out first and fired a few shots at the CCTV monitors. The others weren't too sure.

"No one comes around here. Especially this time of night. And if we fail it won't matter anyway."

He took two more shots at the lock on the doors and led everyone inside.

"Welcome to the best place to hide from the devil."

They looked around, slack jawed. Crates and crates of religious supplies. Everything from Virgin Mary statues, priests' robes, boxes of Bibles, holy water and communion wafers. They looked at Camper for an explanation.

"It's for missionaries, mainly. Everything here is genuine. This isn't just a warehouse of Church of Latter Day Saints fliers. Half of the things in here have actually been blessed. Ready for shipping and ready for use. I've broken in here dozens of times. I think. But the security always remains the same. I don't know. Maybe they do it on purpose. Since I'm not really supposed to exist."

Gamby took Camper's arm and hauled him to one side as the others looked for a place to sit.

"So what's the rest of the plan?"

"Huh?"

"Your plan, Camper. What are we doing here?"

"Um. I didn't actually have one. This place just popped

into my head while we were driving."

"What do you mean it popped into your head?"

"Well, for the first ten minutes I was just following one of the bus routes. Then I thought of it."

Gamby couldn't believe it. Actually, yes. She could.

"So what can we expect? What do you think is going to happen?"

"I don't know. More Hell Hounds maybe? Whoever or whatever killed all those Circle kids probably. Let's hope it's just a normal guy who's been possessed. We can deal with that. I've dealt with it before."

Suddenly Sal's face popped into Camper's head. Sal, and Colt and half a dozen other people he'd forgotten over the years. The little girl.

"So there's a way to reverse possession? You're talking about exorcism right?"

Camper kept his voice low.

"No. I'm not. Exorcism always ends in death. The rite is to cleanse the soul of the possessed, to make it ready for the afterlife. I tend to skip that part."

He put his hand on his hip, where his silver gun was tucked into his pants. Gamby reminded herself again that Camper was a dangerous man and that even good men could be dangerous. Perhaps that's what they needed right now.

The others had hauled some small boxes together to sit on and were talking quietly. Phil found himself pouring over the Charter. He'd gotten over his uneasiness about it and thought maybe he could be of some use. He'd risked so much to get the thing years ago and now here it was. Nothing like he'd imagined. And nothing about real estate. His father would probably be doing the hokey pokey in his grave if he could see it. It read like something out of Evil Dead. And looked it too. The whole thing was written in some poor soul's blood. Phil wondered about the nature of the parchment as well. Something about it didn't feel right. It gave him shivers.

The document was cut and dry. Everything that Camper and Jeremy had told them about it was true. The Dot was a playground for the damned. Hell, it was a theme park. He knew about The Circle now, but he wondered how many other secret groups worked in the city. How many other societies bound to some ancient law? He could always ask Camper, but it looked like he was busy in conversation with the Detective. Probably planning their defense. Against what? This wasn't something they'd be able to handle with a can of peas, that was for sure.

Suddenly there was a noise outside of breaking glass. Everyone jumped. Gamby and Camper both produced their guns. Camper held his in his right hand, his ritual bone in his left. Phil had grabbed the closest statue of the Virgin Mary and was waving it in front of him. Michael had been mediating and nearly knocked over Jeremy when he jumped up at the noise. Camper was the first to move.

"Nobody panic. I've done this before. Dozens of times."

He started to move toward the back of the warehouse.

"It's probably just a cat anyway."

It wasn't a cat.

After a thud and a moan Camper dragged a body back

to the others. It was Malicious, sporting a bump the size of Idaho on his forehead to go along with the one Phil had given him earlier. His hand was bloody too, probably from breaking a window to get in. He would later regret his first hazy words.

"Salacious. You're still alive?"

The punch Gamby landed left him out cold for twenty minutes.

67

Hours earlier, Malicious had woken up inside a broom closet at Phil's American Style Convenience. Things just weren't going his way. Who would have thought that being the head of a Satanic order would be so difficult? It shouldn't have been. He was being tracked. He knew it. The kid. What was his name? Eddie. Eddie Tripper. That was it. Killed off Voracious. And probably the rest of the order. And he's after the Charter. Why would he want it if he was a member of the order itself? It didn't make any sense. And now here he was in a broom closet after getting whacked by a register jockey. Wasn't it supposed to be the other way around?

He got to his feet. That's when he noticed that his briefcase was gone. Must have been the clerk. He looked familiar somehow. Good news was that Eddie wouldn't be tracking him now. Bad news was whatever that clerk had in mind. Couldn't be good. But no one in their right mind would want the Charter destroyed. The city would be in ruins. The demons would be banished. And the devil himself set up the whole deal.

He dusted himself off and kicked the door until it

opened. The store was closed and the clerk was nowhere to be seen. He grabbed a beer from the cooler and went outside. An old dog was making its way down the street. He used to have a dog. Nappy. Wasn't a very energetic dog if he remembered right. Something wrong with him too. Malicious' eyes followed the stray as it wandered down the street. A car drove by. He instantly recognized the face of the man who had locked him up. He jumped into his car and started following. The car was so packed with people in the back that no one noticed him. And for the longest while he felt like he knew where they were going. The route seemed familiar.

68

"The last thing I want to do is defend him, but he *is* after the same thing we are. Protecting the Charter."

Malicious' jaw was swelling up and he could barely hear. There was an argument happening, he knew that. Someone who looked like a cab driver he had once was talking. There was Vanessa Gamby, the damn store clerk, Salacious and Camper King right in the middle of it. Well really. How could Camper King *not* be there? Wait. Didn't he catch him breaking into the place? His head was swimming.

"He's awake. Maybe now we can get some answers."

Camper stood over Malicious.

"So. Who's been killing everyone?"

"Well I can tell you it wasn't me."

Gamby's foot came out of nowhere, kicking him in the ribs before Camper could step in the way.

"You killed Rick! I know it was you, you bastard!"

"Vanessa, I don't think he did."

"Of course it was him. Who else?"

Gamby had her gun out. And she was trembling. Guns and trembling. Always a bad combination. Camper had to defuse the situation quick or they wouldn't be getting any answers.

"Who?"

Malicious rubbed his jaw pretending not to hear. His head was ringing and he needed to figure out how to play this. Fast.

"If you don't tell me who's been killing everyone, then I have no choice but to step aside and let the detective do her job."

Malicious took one look at Gamby and wasted no time.

"Eddie. Eddie Tripper."

"The guy from Three's Company?"

"No. *Eddie* Tripper. He's in The Circle."

"So The Circle is behind it?"

Jeremy came forward.

"No. That doesn't make sense. Why would The Circle order an attack on itself? That can't be it."

"Of course it's not it, *Jeremy*. Eddie Tripper is possessed. I don't know by what. But he seems bent on getting the Charter. I guess you all know that already."

The others shared a knowing look.

"What? Something you're not telling me?"

Gamby put her gun away.

"You're in no position to ask questions. So what do we do, Camper?"

They all looked at him. He'd been working on his own for so long that he was wasn't comfortable in a leadership role. He wasn't ready for it and he didn't want it. But that couldn't be helped now. They had to stay alive. And they had to protect the Charter. He was going to need all their help.

Suddenly Malicious' cell phone started to ring, cutting the tension. Gamby wrestled it out of his pocket and looked at the caller display.

"Well, I'll be damned."

Jeremy leaned over her shoulder.

"Not the most appropriate choice of words. Who is it?"

"Reggie Law."

Jaws dropped one by one. Except for Jeremy, who was still hovering over Gamby's shoulder.

"Are you going to answer it?"

"And say what? Hello Chief, looks like you're friends with a cult leader? Well, I guess I'll hand in my badge tomorrow? I don't think so."

She threw the phone into Malicious' lap.

"What's the story?"

"Not telling."

"You still don't get it do you? I ask the questions and you answer. And keep in mind that this isn't an interrogation room. Anything goes. And I'm just looking for an excuse."

Malicious raised an eyebrow at Jeremy. And Gamby turned her attention.

"Did you know something about this?"

"Well..."

Jeremy had to pick his words carefully here. He wasn't exactly in the detective's good books since Rick had been killed.

"Yes?"

"It's kind of a tradition. The Mayor and the Police

Chief. It goes back since the writing of the Charter. Both positions were sworn to serve The Circle. But not be an actual part of it. Just make their lives a little easier. Some years it doesn't work out. But mostly it does."

"Why didn't you tell me?"

"I didn't see a reason to, yet. And you weren't exactly spilling your beans to the Police Chief, so I didn't see the point. Would he have helped? Maybe. Or maybe he would have had you killed. He has his own agenda. That much I know."

"And what is his agenda? Do you know that?"

"I have no idea. I've never even spoken to the man. Let alone gotten a phone call from him."

Gamby turned again and grabbed Malicious' collar. He winced.

"How about you spill your beans. Before I do it for you."

Before Malicious could answer, a dull thumping started to come from the nearest door and before anyone knew what was happening, Michael took off like a bat out of hell. Nothing but dust and the odor of cheeseburgers in his wake. The thumping got louder and became a chorus of sounds: scraping, pounding and knocking all rolled into one. Camper sprang into action.

"Help me with this crate. The door is locked, but it might not hold for long."

The others, excluding their captured Satanist, helped Camper move a large crate of Bibles in front of the door. The sounds continued, albeit muffled behind the crate. Phil was visibly nervous.

"What do you think is out there?"

Camper played the part of the confident leader. "We'll know soon enough. Once Michael gets back."

"If he's coming back."

"He is. He's out there now. Finding out what's going on. Moving so fast that nobody can even see him."

"If he's moving so fast shouldn't he be back by now?"

Phil's words hit Camper like a ton of wet cement, but he made sure not to show it.

"He'll be back. He might have gone for help."

Phil almost asked him who Micheal was going to find. Who could possibly help them? Let alone believe them? But he didn't. He could see the wheels turning in Camper's mind, trying to figure out the situation. He'd come up with something. He had to.

Minutes went by. And those minutes turned into a half hour. The thumping continued and Camper and the others had to barricade three more doors. No one spoke about Michael. Although they all secretly wondered how he would get back in if all the doors were barred.

An hour went by. Gamby had taken to checking the warehouse inch by inch, while Camper and Jeremy poured over the Charter looking for something. Anything. Phil sat on the floor, keeping watch over their prisoner. Malicious just sat there waiting for something to happen.

And then just like that something happened.

There was the sound of broken glass and Michael came tearing into the room. His arms were cut and he looked like he had just spent the last twelve hours digging ditches. He took one look at everyone, tried to speak, and then fell to the floor. Camper was the first at his side.

"Michael? Michael, wake up."

He slowly came to. His eyes were bloodshot and he was having trouble breathing.

"Had to come back. You're not going to believe it."

"Try me."

"How about this? Army of the dead."

Camper swore to himself.

"Zombies. Damn it."

Phil was dumbfounded.

"Did I hear you right? Did you say zombies? You're kidding right?"

"No. I'm not. That's what's been trying to get in through the doors. How did you get in Michael?"

"Ran up the side of the building. Went in through a window and ran down the other side."

Gamby's eyes went wide.

"Easy when you know how. But I don't think I'll be running again tonight. Or all week for that matter."

"Just take it easy for a bit. We're going to handle this. But first I need you to tell me everything you saw."

69

Michael had been one of those kids who spent too much time by himself. Sitting alone in his room and daydreaming. He had learned to run in high school. There was a story on the news about a man who had gone missing in the woods west of the city. Michael went out looking for him and found the body, face down in a creek. He was so spooked that he ran. And when he finally stopped running, out of breath and exhilarated, he was three states away. Having to call his Dad from Wyoming for a ride home was not a pleasant experience. He spent the next three months grounded. Normally he wouldn't care, but something was happening to him and he wanted to get out and experiment with it. He spent his time trying to remember how he felt when he found the body and what had triggered his running. Weeks went by and when his punishment was over he put on his best pair of sneakers and ran to Mexico and back. It was after this that the Doctor found him. And his time in the service of The Society for the Recognition of Meta States had begun.

70

"Michael?"

Camper was leaning over him, worry and confusion on his face.

"Camper?"

"That's right. You passed out again."

"How many times is that?"

"Four."

"If it gets to eight I'm going home."

He giggled. His brain felt mushy. He had pushed himself way too hard out there. Something was bound to happen on the inside.

"What happened out there?"

"There was a kid."

Michael blinked a few times, trying to clear the cobwebs.

"A kid. I think he was in control. He knew I was there. He couldn't see me. But he knew. I think he tried to get into my head."

Camper stood up suddenly. He shared a look with Jeremy.

"What is it Camper? He didn't get in. Don't worry

about that."

Jeremey stepped forward and looked Michael straight in the eye.

"What happened to Eddie? The kid, what happened to him?"

"It was awful. He fell to the ground. They surrounded him. I don't know what happened after that, but you can imagine."

Camper didn't like where this was going. He didn't like it at all. A choice was coming. He could feel it. If Eddie had died, the zombies should have crumbled. They needed a mind in control of them. Whatever had been in control of Eddie had moved on. Found someone else. Someone close by. But without a place of possession it shouldn't have been possible. Unless...

"Camper!"

King looked up. Phil was looking at the Charter. He had seen something that might help. Or at least he thought it might. The others gathered around.

"This section here. It's an amendment. Look. The color of the ink, the blood, is different. It's not as faded."

"Are you telling me we could just write an amendment to this thing and be done with it?"

"It's not that easy."

The voice was Michael. But twisted and not quite his own. Camper knew right away what it meant. He suspected it. They turned around. Micheal was on his feet, as though nothing had happened to him. But his eyes were glossy.

"That's right Camper. I'm in here. Not my first time inside a human capable of meta states, but it's always interesting. This body isn't in much condition to do anything right now, but give me a few minutes and we'll see."

Gamby took out her gun.

"Oh that's not necessary, Vanessa. I'd just jump into someone else. That wouldn't be very nice now, would it?"

Gamby lowered her weapon. Everyone's eyes were fixed on Michael. And what was inside him.

"I've got a proposition. Let's end all this. You don't want to see your city go up in flames. We amend the Charter. Dissolve The Circle. They obviously weren't doing their jobs. We come to a new arrangement."

Camper was hesitant.

"What kind of arrangement?"

Micheal's voice made the others sick. It hung in the air like a disease.

"As long as the greater demons of hell are fighting, I am in control. The harder it is for them to get souls, the harder they fight. The better for me. I thought to lock them out entirely, destroy the contract and let their war end. But it's been such a good war. It would be a shame to end it just when it's getting interesting. I'm offering you a choice. Amend the Charter here and now, or I follow you to the ends of the Earth until it, and your city, is in flames."

Phil couldn't believe they were actually listening to this. But Camper picked up the Charter and walked toward Michael.

"What kind of amendment?"

"Well, I hear you're out of a job?"

This was getting worse by the minute. It was gonna go

bad no matter what.

"Out with it."

Gamby's face dropped.

"You can't be serious."

"We don't have much of a choice."

The thing inside Michael smiled.

"The human world has had you for long enough. I'm not really proposing anything too radical. Your job stays the same. Just a little change in management."

Phil could see the look in Camper's eyes. He was considering it.

"Talk."

A sick grin spread across Micheal's face.

"Now that's what I like to hear. You'll be working for me, Camper. As long as they keep fighting, I win. And if you're up here preventing them from getting what they want, well then they'll just keep fighting and bickering among themselves trying to get it. And that's exactly how I like it."

"And what happens if they get what they're looking for?"

At this point no one even wanted to say the word *souls* because a soul meant a life. And bargaining for those wasn't right. The thing inside Michael sensed the uneasiness. He stretched, casually, like a house cat. A very dangerous one.

"Well, if any one dies then it's your fault, Camper. But a lot more will die if we don't make this deal."

There it was in black and white and red all over. A deal. A deal with the devil. And he was actually considering it.

"The Hanged Man wants me dead."

Michael laughed. It sounded like someone eating styrofoam.

"Everyone wants you dead."

Malicious looked up at him.

"He's got a point there."

Gamby shot him a look that would tear a hole in the ozone. Camper stepped forward.

"So what happens?"

Gamby wasn't the only one to speak, but she was the loudest.

"You can't be serious! Camper this isn't right! We can-"

"What, Gamby? Vanessa. This is the best thing to do. For The Dot and for everyone in it. It's the only way."

He turned back to Michael.

"So?"

Michael reached out his hand for the Charter. Camper slowly walked forward. Phil started to sweat abnormally. Malicious unconsciously shifted away from the action. Jeremy and Gamby looked at each other and then back to Camper, expecting a last minute move or trick to come running down his sleeve. But it didn't.

Michael held the Charter in his hand, gave it a quick once over and then laid it on a table, motioning to Camper to come over.

"I'll need a little of your blood to seal the deal."

Camper wasn't giving in without some details first.

"I want to know exactly what will happen. No double talk. No lies."

At the word *lies* Michael cracked another of those sickening grins.

"I'm contracting you to hunt down any greater demons or their agents who are working in The Dot. In addition, you'll be above their influence. No more manipulating. Hunt them down, send them back to me and the war keeps going. The Charter with the city remains intact, amended of course, and the city stays safe from collapse."

Camper looked Michael in the eye.

"You don't get my soul."

Michael laughed again. It filled the warehouse, shaking dust from the roof.

"Of course not. But don't worry. I'll be trying for that eventually."

"And my friends?"

He couldn't even believe he was saying the word. It felt good. The only friend he really had was Sal. And the Hanged Man had taken care of that. Maybe this deal wasn't so bad. It would be nice to get some payback.

"They go back to their own lives. You can use them as you wish. As allies, or as shields. It's up to you. I'll leave this body intact if you're worried about it. Pick one of them to carry the Charter. Since I've dissolved The Circle it will need a new guardian. Now, how about that blood?"

Camper rolled up his sleeve. He looked over at his friends. No one tried to stop him. They all knew this was the best and only way. Gamby's eyes were filling. Camper couldn't help but think of a hockey draft and himself as the number one pick. He should have held out for more. Michael produced a pen from somewhere and flicked it across Camper's arm. Blood trickled down to his hand. He worked quickly, writing out the contract that would put Camper on the other team. Camper looked down at the document and faces flashed before his eyes of all the people he had wronged, all the deaths that he had failed to prevent and all the ones that he had caused. In his mind's eye he saw the little girl. She looked at him without smiling. Her eyes bored into his head and then she nodded slowly and faded away.

And then, without any pomp or circumstance, without any flashing lights or raging hellfire, Camper signed on the dotted line.

There was no immediate effect of the signing. Michael waved it around like a Polaroid waiting for the blood to dry.

"Detective Gamby? You'll find that Reggie Law has killed himself when you go back to work tomorrow. No big deal. He wasn't a very nice man. And hey, maybe you could apply for the job."

Gamby sat down. This was all getting to be a little too much.

"The Mayor will be next. A week from today. In his bathroom. Ah, don't worry about it, he wasn't friends with any of you."

This whole time Malicious had been slowly creeping his way along the floor looking for cover. If The Circle was being dissolved, he was next for disintegration.

"It's alright *Malicious.* I've got some work for you down south."

His mouth dropped.

"No. Not *that* down south. You'll like it. Just a little pet project. There will be a ticket on your kitchen counter tomorrow morning. I'd advise you to take it."

He smiled again and handed the Charter to Camper.

"Well, I guess that's the end of our little palaver. Camper, you won't remember any of this, but I'm sure you're friends will fill you in later."

"What do you mean I won't remember...?"

And just like that he was gone. Camper caught Michael as he fell to the ground. A few minutes later he woke up. Nothing but a headache and an empty stomach. He smiled slightly.

"I'm starved."

71

A few days later Camper had forgotten almost everything that had happened. He woke up, had some cereal and turned on some cartoons. His message machine was blinking. He didn't even know he *had* a message machine. Of course he didn't even remember shaving his head, so that was nothing new. One message was from a Father Eric. Something about rebuilding St. Pat's Church. He was pretty sure he didn't know a Father Eric, but was excited about the Church being rebuilt. He remembered it had burned down recently and that was a shame. The second message was from Police Chief Gamby. That was odd. Really damn odd. Absolutely no reason for the chief of police to be calling him. It made him nervous, considering his line of work. He sat back, crunched his cereal and let the message play out. It had filled the rest of the tape. Quite an eye opener. Among other things the message told him the name of the guy sleeping on his couch. Jeremy. And that he used to be a Satanist.

Suddenly he heard a car horn from outside. He looked out the window and saw a cab pulled up to the curb. The cabby waved at him to come out. Camper grabbed his coat without thinking and headed out the door.

It was going to be an interesting day.

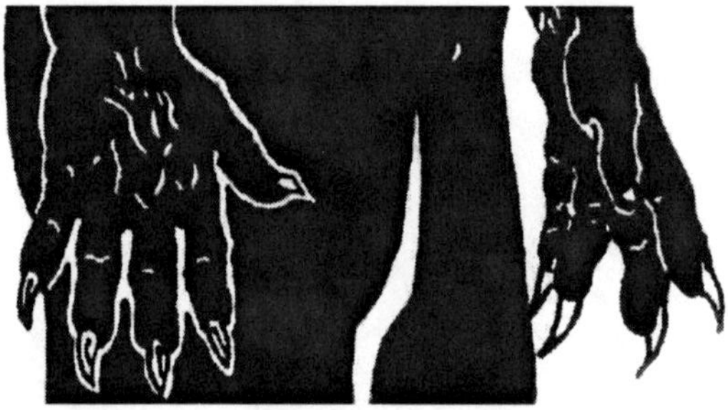

Author Photo: Doug Allen

ABOUT THE AUTHOR

Kevin Woolridge was born in 1977 in St. John's, Newfoundland.

He holds a BFA (theatre) from Grenfell College.

When not writing, he spends his time working as an actor/musician for various theatre companies, and drawing his comic book series *The Little World*.

The Man With The Hole in His Head is his first novel.

CPSIA information can be obtained at www.ICGtesting.com
Printed in the USA
LVOW060528090413

328188LV00001B/4/P

9 781926 903088